JUSTICIAR

THE VIGILANTE CHRONICLES™ BOOK FIVE

NATALIE GREY

MICHAEL ANDERLE

DISRUPTIVE IMAGINATION

THE JUSTICIAR TEAM

Thanks to our JIT Readers

John Ashmore
Kelly O'Donnell
Nicole Emens
Mary Morris
Daniel Weigert
Keith Verret
Peter Manis
Paul Westman

If We've missed anyone, please let us know!

Editor
Lynne Stiegler

From Natalie

For M and T

From Michael

To Family, Friends and
Those Who Love
To Read.
May We All Enjoy Grace
To Live The Life We Are
Called.

CHAPTER ONE

Thirty minutes out from the stranded ship, Shinigami reported.

"Heading to the bridge." Barnabas whistled as he made his way through the white corridors of the *Shinigami*. The ship raced through a particularly lonely patch of what Shinigami had nicknamed "the Jellyfish Sector."

The name referred to one of the more noteworthy races in this area of space, the Jotun. They looked like multicolored blobs of jelly and tended to transport themselves around in mechanical suits with a range of intriguing features.

Barnabas had worked with some of the Jotun Navy in his last mission, which had given him a great deal of respect for the Jotuns as a species and an absolute hatred of the Jotun Parliament.

Corrupt bastards, the lot of them. They had signed their people over to a bloodthirsty corporation in return for a few beach houses and Lord only knew what other trinkets. Shinigami had uncovered enough dirty money trails running through their system that Barnabas could have made nearly every member of Parliament a pariah in society. He hadn't released the information yet, but he fully intended to if they pissed him off in the future.

Shinigami had accused him of blackmail. Barnabas maintained it wasn't blackmail if they didn't *know* his plan. Gar and Tafa, meanwhile, had wisely opted not to weigh in.

Barnabas turned a corner and gave a yell as he tripped over a body. Eyes stared sightlessly at the ceiling while pale hands lay palm up, fingers slightly curled.

Ghostly snickering echoed from the nearby speakers. "You look ridiculous," Shinigami told Barnabas in deep amusement.

"For the *last* time…" Barnabas recovered his footing and adjusted his vest, glaring at the speakers, "do *not* leave your body in the corridor. You have rooms of your own now. You pestered me about them for *days*."

"I need clothes."

"No, you don't. You don't use your body." Barnabas hauled the limp thing up by the armpits and dragged it to the side of the corridor.

"I do too!"

"Then I don't suppose you'd help me with this? Mechanical bodies are heavy."

"You could use the exercise. Too much fruit juice."

"Low." Barnabas knew she was only teasing. With his upgrades, he was practically incapable of carrying extra weight. Still, Shinigami had discovered something that he had managed to hide from nearly everyone else: he was incredibly vain. She needled him about it at regular intervals, making fun of his hair, his clothing and now his looks. He smoothed a hand over his stomach and glared at the speakers again. "And you're hardly one to get on my case about exercise. How long since you last used this body?"

Shinigami flickered into being as a projection. With her arms crossed and one hip jutted out, she looked unimpressed.

"It is not the same thing at all. I don't need to work my muscles or increase my cardiovascular function."

"On the contrary." Barnabas leaned forward with a smile. "It's *very* similar. You, like anyone in training, need to learn to make your body do what you want it to. You need to learn to interpret its feedback. You find this process frustrating, as we do. Therefore…" His smile broadened, and he shrugged slightly, "you slack."

Shinigami's face turned stony. "I am not *slacking*. I am flying this ship!"

"Says an AI who once told me that she had plenty of capacity to handle multiple projects at once. Are you running out of memory? Do you need a defrag?" Barnabas took pleasure in waltzing directly through Shinigami's projection.

"Listen, you ingrate, I am not going to take this abuse from you!"

"Mmmhmm. Well, may I remind you that you very much wanted to—what was it you said, exactly?—ah, yes 'smash some skulls in.'" Barnabas cast a look over his shoulder.

"I can do that!"

"You definitely cannot. I am not letting you off this ship and into combat until *I* think you're ready."

Shinigami created another projection right in front of him, causing him to stop briefly on instinct. She snickered at his expression. "Ah, yes, the much-vaunted human intellect. We're *much* better off with you in charge."

"Let's try that experiment with *you*," Barnabas muttered. "You'll trip over your own feet."

"I will not. This body is an atrocity and is far too difficult to use."

"So we'll take the body back," Barnabas said airily.

"No! It's mine."

"You don't want it, and I'm sure Achronyx could use one."

Shinigami huffed but did not answer. A moment later, Barnabas heard a sound behind him. He turned to see the body come to life. It was always a somewhat disturbing process to watch it animate, and he grimaced when the chest shuddered and the eyes blinked.

It took two tries for Shinigami to get up off the floor. "This is harder for me than you," she complained to Barnabas. "AIs aren't meant to have to learn this sort of thing."

"You *wanted* to learn this," Barnabas pointed out. He made sure not to let his face twitch with amusement while the body walked jerkily toward him. "Besides, you have far more memory to create things like subroutines. You can build an entirely new way of learning to use a body. And have you *seen* little kids learning to walk before? They're not good at it."

"I saw holos of Christina— "

"Christina doesn't count."

They made their way to the bridge, Barnabas ambling with his hands in his pockets, Shinigami swearing both out of the speakers and the mechanical body as she struggled to walk smoothly.

Barnabas refrained from suggesting she speak to Jeltor. He had mentioned it already, and Shinigami had been resistant to the idea of, as she said, "Having a jellyfish teach me how to walk." Barnabas thought Jeltor was probably the *best* person to teach her, but he was trying to learn to keep his mouth shut.

He wasn't very good at it yet.

On the bridge, he found Tafa sitting at the navigator's desk watching the charted route and making minute adjustments. She flashed them both a smile.

"I thought you said *you* were flying the ship," Barnabas said to Shinigami.

"I'm backup," Shinigami replied, with great dignity. "Tafa doesn't know all the ins and outs of the ship's capabilities yet."

"Mmm." Barnabas thought Tafa was showing an innate grasp of the skill, but he did not voice that thought. He took a seat in the captain's chair and watched while Shinigami struggled to sit gracefully in the next chair over. "You're getting better at that."

"I still tip at the end." She sounded disgruntled. "How do you all avoid doing that?"

"It has to do with the balance of the weight and committing to the movement."

"Show me," Shinigami ordered.

With a roll of his eyes, Barnabas complied, standing up and sitting down several times while Shinigami watched.

When he finished, he sat down and crossed his legs,

only to jump as Gar's voice said, "What in the sea was *that* all about?"

"Shinigami is learning how to sit." Barnabas looked over as Gar joined them. Gar prided himself on being more cosmopolitan than most Luvendi, who were famously insular. He was also a good deal less amoral than many others of his species who had left their home planet.

Still, the more comfortable he became with his new shipmates, the more Luvendi colloquialisms peppered his speech. Using "the sea" when others might use "the universe" was one of them—a giant ocean covered Luvendan, and the Luvendi lived in giant submerged towers.

Gar sat on Barnabas' left, unaware of Shinigami leaning forward to watch.

"He's more graceful than you are," Shinigami told Barnabas, needling him again with a wicked grin.

"Mainly because I have spent most of my life worried that my bones would fracture if I weren't careful," Gar pointed out. Tall and thin, he nonetheless had muscle tone that no other Luvendi in the universe could claim. Shinigami had modified him in the Pod-doc, increasing his bone strength—Luvendi were famously fragile—and increasing his healing speed and his reflexes, and enhancing his senses.

Now, unaware of the argument going on under the surface of the conversation, Gar nodded at the screen. "Any more details on the stranded ship?"

"Only a few," Shinigami reported. "I ran what I could through the reports from local stations. If it's the ship I think it is, it's civilian. Has a large cargo hold, probably for food transport as a side business but is mainly for passengers. Lots of bunks."

"No word on the nature of the emergency?" Barnabas had picked up the distress call a few days earlier while attending a celebration of the defeat of the Yennai Corporation. Since the ship was stranded in a very remote area, he had decided to pursue the lead.

After all, it was unlikely that anyone else could get to them faster than the *Shinigami* could. With the best of Etheric Empire technology, the ship had the security features necessary to venture into an area potentially filled with pirates.

In all honesty, Barnabas was hoping they would encounter a few. He was longing for a nice uncomplicated bit of work, something that *didn't* involve massive shadowy corporations that had infiltrated multiple governments and business sectors.

Perhaps someone on the ship would have a good lead to follow.

Shinigami's face went blank. While she had learned the knack of emoting with her projections, she still did not think to do so when she was inhabiting her new mechanical body. "I'm picking something up," she said in an emotionless voice.

She brought the disturbance up on the screen, and everyone frowned and leaned forward to look.

The ship most likely thought it was invisible to the *Shinigami's* detection. It was approaching from a nearby cloud of debris, which Shinigami now scanned. The scan turned up pieces of two distinct ships, one Brakalon and one Shrillexian.

"The wrecks are recent," she told Barnabas.

Barnabas sat back with a frown. "What do you think the odds are," he asked no one in particular, "that a ship hiding here with two recent wrecks is *not* connected to the ship making the distress call?"

There was a silence. Tafa, who had not been involved in any of their combat missions before, was staring at the screen with wide eyes. Gar looked intrigued, and Shinigami still looked blank as she sorted through data.

Finally, and somewhat mechanically, she turned her head to look at Barnabas. Her features were a mix of Bethany Anne's and Tabitha's, but the feral grin was entirely her own.

"Shall we say hello?" she asked sweetly.

Barnabas grinned back. "It would only be polite."

CHAPTER TWO

"Hail them." Barnabas nodded at the ship on the screen. "And tell me as soon as you know anything about where this ship originated."

He was curious. It was a type of ship he had never seen before—a light, sleek scouting vessel, perhaps. The wreckage of the other ships, however, suggested that this ship had more weapons than most scouts Barnabas had seen.

They had taken down a Shrillexian vessel, after all, and you couldn't do that without some combination of skill and weaponry. Shrillexians had fully *earned* the hatred they received from other species—they weren't slouches in the fighting department.

Shinigami's avatar would have nodded, but her body didn't yet. She was spending all her energy hitting the buttons to hail the other ship with her actual fingers rather than using her internal processes.

As a result, Barnabas and Gar were both still craning to

look at her hand when the holo connected. Both sat up, Barnabas clearing his throat self-consciously and Gar crossing his legs in a vague mimicry of Barnabas. He also tried to clear his throat, but the sound came out sort of like a hiccup. Barnabas felt his lips twitch and hoped he didn't look too undignified.

He peered at the darkness of the screen. "Shinigami, the call hasn't connected."

"The connection is—"

"I do not wish to be seen," the pilot of the other ship said. Barnabas guessed that the voice had been run through several filters to distort it, because it was oddly mechanical. "How are you seeing my ship?"

"Oh," Barnabas asked innocently, "was it cloaked?"

Gar gave a snort and pressed his lips shut to hold back more laughter.

On the other end, there was a cold pause. "Leave this area," the pilot ordered finally. "This will be your only warning."

"Why do we need to leave?" Barnabas was quite enjoying acting oblivious. He painted a look of concern on his face.

"I have ordered you to leave. As I said, there will be no further warnings."

"Yes, but *who* is ordering us?" The words didn't have quite the same aura of innocence to them this time. Barnabas did not like the tone of the phrase, "I have ordered you."

There was another pause. "I have ordered you to leave," the pilot repeated.

Barnabas tried a different tack. "We can't leave, unfortunately. We're responding to a distress call."

"I responded to that call." The answer was too quick, and even through the language barrier and the various filters, it had the cadence of someone telling a lie. "The situation has been resolved. As you can see, the distress signal has stopped broadcasting."

"On the contrary," Shinigami interjected. She had perfected a single posture: straight-backed, with her hands on the arms of the chair and her legs crossed, and, since she never slipped out of that posture or slouched, she looked like a queen.

Barnabas guessed it was something she had learned from watching Bethany Anne interact with people. Bethany Anne might despise the tedium of court appearances and the uselessness of political wrangling, but one thing was certain: she knew how to make an impression, and she *did*.

"The distress signal is still being broadcast," Shinigami confirmed now. Her face did not change as she spoke, and she forgot to blink. It was fascinating to watch. "However, the signal is being blocked by a network of devices that share programming similarities with your ship."

The answer did not come in words. Instead, a pair of missiles appeared on the *Shinigami's* sensors in a storm of beeps. A map of the two projectiles replaced the dark holoscreen, and a touchscreen swung from Gar's chair for him to coordinate a response. He looked at Shinigami for the go-ahead.

"I've taken care of— Dammit." The speakers cut off, and

Shinigami used the body instead. She turned her head somewhat unnaturally. "I've taken care of it," she told Gar.

"You *have* to blink," Barnabas said. "It's making *my* eyes sting at this point. Just put a subroutine in there or something."

"I'd like to point out that you've gotten a lot more confident in my ship-to-ship combat skills if this is what you're focusing on."

"Yes, well, you taking out three ships in orbit around High Tortuga made quite an impression. *Blink.*" Barnabas shook himself and blinked several times for good measure. He looked at the screen, where the two missiles were still showing up. "You said you took care of them?"

"I did." Shinigami managed a smile and turned her head back to watch the screen.

Closer, the projectiles raced, and closer. Their speed did not alter in the slightest and Barnabas had the sudden thought that he had not felt the *Shinigami* disgorge weapons of its own. It was a well-constructed ship, but still, one could always feel a faint tremor when missiles or countermeasures launched.

"Um," Gar said faintly, "Shinigami..."

"Wait for it," Shinigami said sweetly.

Gar made a gesture that Barnabas guessed was the equivalent of crossing himself. Meanwhile, on the screen, the ship had changed its cloaking algorithms and was flickering on and off the sensor net as it slid into the blackness. Doubtless, it thought that the crew of the *Shinigami* had not yet noticed the missiles and would soon be dead.

Barnabas found it difficult to argue with that assessment at present.

"Shinigami?"

"Keep waiting."

"Shinigami, is this so that you won't have to spend time learning to walk?"

Shinigami said nothing.

The beeping was nearly constant now as the missiles hurtled closer, and despite himself, Barnabas was beginning to sweat a little. "I'm not going to give your body to Achronyx! That was a joke!"

Shinigami flipped her hair out of the way and leaned on one elbow, putting her chin on her fist.

"You can't blink, but you can do *that*?" Barnabas demanded. "Why is this going to be the last conversation I have before I die? *Shinigami*, for the love of all that is holy—"

The beeping stopped. Barnabas squeezed his eyes shut, waiting for the explosion to tear through the ship, and a moment later cracked one eye open to look around.

"Shinigami..."

"The missiles are not on the scanners," Gar reported. He sounded hesitant, as though he might be misinterpreting the completely blank screen. Understandable, in Barnabas' opinion.

"Yes, we see things as the other ship sees them. Or, more accurately..." Shinigami brought up a report on the screen. There was the fading heat signature of an explosion and shattered pieces of metal and plastic swirling.

"You...made him think we're dead?" Barnabas felt the engines kick in. "What are we doing now?"

"Surprising him. I want to see his face."

"And you didn't tell us you were doing this because..."

She looked at him as though he were a complete idiot. "Because I wanted to see *your* faces."

Barnabas considered this as the ship maneuvered. He sat back in his chair, tapping his fingers on the arm. "I'm going to get you for that."

"How? Are you going to send me to my room without dinner? Will I have to mow the whole lawn, Grandpa?"

Barnabas' face went stony. The sound of Tafa giggling in the background did nothing to improve his mood. The alien ship replaced the false images on the screen, sliding and jumping. The cameras could not seem to get a good fix on where it was. He could only hope that Shinigami *did*.

A moment later, however, he grinned when the ship swung around hard, and Shinigami said, with feeling, "*Boo, motherfucker!*"

They must have been hooked into the audio from the other ship because there was a sudden storm of cursing. Shinigami's face went blank as she tried to interpret the words.

"Jotun, I think," she told Barnabas in an undertone. "As for the make of the ship, I got *nothing*. It shares characteristics with any number of species' ships."

"Jotun?" Barnabas' eyebrows shot up. *That* was interesting—and it was something he intended to ask Jeltor about as soon as they were out of this mess. He added equally quietly, "Dare I ask—where *are* the missiles?"

"Oh, *that*." Shinigami wiggled her fingers.

"Seriously, you know jazz hands, but you don't blink?"

"At this point, I'm not blinking because it annoys the crap out of you."

Barnabas sank his head into one hand and groaned softly.

"The missiles are circling toward his ship." Shinigami abruptly remembered to grin. The sudden change was terrifying.

"Ah." Barnabas looked at the screen. "As you may be aware, there are two missiles headed toward you. Be so good as to answer some questions, and we *may* deal with them for you."

"Who the *hell* are you?" the alien demanded.

"No, I said *answer* some questions, not *ask* them."

"Leave this place!"

"He's not very good at this, is he?" Barnabas asked generally. He focused on the dark screen once more. "So, you're Jotun. Why are you hiding here trying to kill the ships responding to distress calls?"

There was stony silence, and then the ship tipped up and accelerated away sharply. With a whoop, Shinigami gave chase.

"I *love* it when they run!"

"Are you descended from coyotes? And keep the channel open."

Shinigami shot him a grin as she guided the ship through a series of tight twists and turns to follow the escaping Jotun. She was no longer even pretending to use her body to give the commands. She had adopted one of Bethany Anne's signature poses again, sitting at attention and swaying slightly as Shinigami used her computers to maneuver more tightly than any human could have.

"You seem to be having some trouble," Barnabas remarked to the Jotun. He thought he heard another muttered oath. "As you see, you can't get away from us. I don't necessarily want you to die, simply answer some questions. The ship that's waiting out there is still broadcasting its distress signal. If you didn't want it broadcasting, why not simply destroy it?"

There was no answer.

Barnabas rolled his eyes and looked heavenward, praying for patience. "If you *want* to die for this, you can, but I admit I'm curious. What could be—"

Shinigami gave a yell, and their ship veered sideways. Barnabas gave her a confused look that disappeared a moment later when the Jotun's ship exploded in a white-hot blaze.

"Were those its missiles?" He looked at her. "Because I think we could have—"

"No." She gave him what Tabitha called "a Look with a capital L." "Give me a little credit; I wouldn't have blown him up while he still might have talked. No, he did that to himself. He set off a self-destruct." She shrugged. "Or she, I guess. I couldn't run a reverse on all of the voice modifiers."

"They *killed* themselves?" Barnabas looked at the screen incredulously. "Rather than answer a few questions about..." His voice trailed off, and he frowned.

He did not like this in the slightest. What was on that civilian transport that could cause an unaffiliated assassin to destroy rescue ships?

"We had better find out what's going on," Barnabas remarked coldly.

"I agree." Shinigami looked vaguely regretful. "Too bad

he didn't stay around a while longer. I was almost into his systems."

"Whatever we find on the transport ship may give us the answers we need." Barnabas shook his head.

He wasn't particularly hopeful, however—and he wasn't looking forward to this mission anymore, either. What had seemed like a nice, simple rescue operation was quickly becoming quite a bit more complicated.

CHAPTER THREE

D espite its name, the *Srisa* was registered to a Brakalon corporation, and thus—apparently— subject to Brakalon law. In this case, the law stated that the engines must be cut, and the ship must come to a complete stop until the legal issue on board was resolved.

"Legal issue?" Barnabas asked the captain delicately. He peered into the captain's mind, but the thoughts he saw were not entirely clear: a smashed jar of some kind, a Jotun, and a mess of the usual things that would occur to a captain, such as low food stores and angry passengers. The captain was also on his guard when it came to Barnabas, viewing him as a potential threat.

Barnabas supposed that was fair. Piracy was a big industry in almost all sectors. Several people had tried to take the *Shinigami*, and it wasn't unheard of for pirates to talk their way onto ships. The captain must feel like a sitting duck.

"Err..." The captain, Kelnamon, gave a pained-looking smile and scratched his collar nervously. He was an unusual shade of greenish brown. Barnabas could not determine if that was due to long hours inside the ship, or simply a Brakalon ethnic group he had not come across before.

Kelnamon took his time answering. He peered at Barnabas. He shook his head side to side a few times.

Finally, he said, "We should speak alone."

Barnabas gave a gracious nod and prayed for patience, motioning for Gar to stay and Shinigami to come with him. They had arranged this in advance. Shinigami would accompany Barnabas and might be able to unravel any secrets within the *Srisa's* systems, and Gar and Tafa would pretend to wait docilely by the airlock until Barnabas was out of sight, after which they would set about exploring the ship.

Shinigami had wanted to explore, but Tafa had observed that there were still some issues with Shinigami's body doing things like walking. Navigating an unfamiliar ship full of ladders and unusual surfaces was going to enhance Shinigami's jerky movements and tip people off that she wasn't an organic life form.

Shinigami had acceded but had kept up a steady stream of muttering in Barnabas' head even as she stalked along beside him. Barnabas meanwhile looked around and felt vaguely out of scale. The *Srisa* had been built with Brakalons in mind, and the corridors dwarfed most other species. Only Gar seemed tall enough, and the ship's size made him appear even more unnaturally thin than usual.

The captain's chambers were lived-in, but there was no luxury. It was a matter of small touches: carved icons along the metal beams, a hand-stitched blanket on the bed, a rag rug that fit the unusual shape of the floor exactly.

Barnabas had a much better opinion of Kelnamon after seeing this. Many captains became despots, glorying in their tiny realm and wanting to rule with an iron fist, and they invariably shoved as many luxuries as they could into their lives. He hadn't gotten a striking sense of self-importance from Kelnamon so far, but a fleeting glimpse into someone's mind wouldn't always give the whole picture. This cabin helped flesh things out.

"So," Barnabas leaned against the wall, one eyebrow raised, "what's the legal issue?"

The Brakalon groaned and rubbed his temples. "I shouldn't say. It needs to be handled by the authorities. They were supposed to arrive yesterday."

Barnabas and Shinigami exchanged a look. They had seen the wreckage of the Brakalon ship, and now they knew why one had arrived so quickly.

Barnabas cleared his throat. "I'm afraid that ship isn't coming. There was interference." He tried to keep his voice light to avoid making things sound too meaningful. He did not particularly want to get caught up in the story of the ship they had encountered—not until they knew what was happening with the *Srisa*, at any rate.

"What do you mean it's not coming?" Kelnamon looked at him worriedly.

"It's like this," Shinigami said.

Shinigami—

No, I got this, it's cool.

"It's cool"?

Yeah. It's cool. She tossed her dark hair over her shoulder and gave the Brakalon captain a grimace. "That Brakalon police ship? It's in lots of little pieces with some other ships *also* in lots of little pieces. About half an hour..." She considered, looking around, and then pointed. "That way."

Most people don't know that sort of thing off-hand, and why did he need to know the direction?

I don't know what information you people find useful.

You're insane. Also, your bedside manner needs work.

Who's at a bedside?

It's an expression.

Kelnamon, unaware of the conversation going on between the two of them, looked alarmed. "You saw it?" His eyes narrowed. "Or..."

"We had nothing to do with the accident," Barnabas assured him. He gave Shinigami a severe look. *Behave yourself.* "We were surprised that there was another ship already here, given how remote you were. This explains why the ship was there, but I'm afraid it doesn't explain why it was destroyed."

The Brakalon went an even more sickly shade of brownish green. It must be a sign of stress, Barnabas decided. Kelnamon began to pace around his little patch of the room.

"We don't have enough supplies to stay here much longer. We have to get this cleared up."

"Mmm. Well, given that your friends won't be arriving anytime soon, perhaps you could tell us what's going on?" Barnabas gave him a pleasant schmoozing-over-martinis sort of smile. "After all, I have some legal credentials."

And you call me clueless, Shinigami commented.

What?

You think that's going to win you any friends?

He needs police. We're...kind of police.

He's nervous, you were a Ranger, *and you radiate that you're going to cause massive trouble wherever you go.*

I do not!

You do. But don't take my word for it. See what he says. She didn't look at Barnabas, but her face glowed with self-satisfied pleasure.

She had a point, in that the captain looked nervous rather than reassured. Kelnamon was wringing his hands, and finally said, "What sort of legal experience?" His tone sounded like he was expecting to hear Barnabas admit to going around lopping people's heads off at the drop of a hat.

Go on, Shinigami urged wickedly, *Tell him.*

I'm not sure this is a good idea.

She was grinning like a Cheshire Cat by now, and Barnabas wished he hadn't said anything. He had no choice, however. He met the captain's eyes and gave a small shrug. "Before the Etheric Empire disbanded, I was one of the Empress' Rangers."

"He was Ranger *One*," Shinigami clarified.

The Brakalon looked more nervous than ever. "This is Brakalon business. There's no reason the Etheric Empire has to get involved."

"There is no Etheric Empire anymore," Barnabas explained. "I am no longer an instrument of the Empress' Justice, but instead of...Justice in general." When Kelnamon looked blankly at him, he clarified: "I travel, find issues that require intervention, and aid anyone who needs me. At present, it seems like you need someone."

The captain looked like a very massive deer caught in headlights.

Barnabas fought the urge to sigh deeply. He drew himself up, smiled his best do-not-even-think-of-weaseling-out-of-this smile, and asked, "So what's going on?"

Kelnamon was startled into speech. Barnabas' question didn't offer the possibility of turning down help, and in any case, the captain *was* desperate. He dropped into his chair—which creaked ominously—and began, "One of the passengers was murdered."

Oh, now this *is interesting,* Shinigami commented.

You can say that again. Barnabas kept his face from showing any emotion and nodded for the captain to continue, moving to take the other chair.

What he did *not* do was waste time feigning shock and horror. Most people would, and Kelnamon might allow his emotions to get the better of him, allowing not only shock to overwhelm him, but also fear about allowing Barnabas to intervene. At Barnabas's nod, however, the captain shook himself and simply continued with the tale.

"It happened in his cabin. A crew member went to clean the room, and he was dead. It was neatly done. Someone had gone through his things."

"You say, 'Neatly done.' Tell me about that." Barnabas was intrigued.

"The wires that held—well, he was Jotun. I should mention that, or it won't make sense."

Coincidence? Barnabas asked. A Jotun dead, and another hiding near the place of the murder dispatching anyone who might try to investigate.

Shinigami didn't even bother responding to such an obvious question.

Kelnamon gave a few half-hearted attempts at explaining power sources and electronic systems and finally gave up. "His suit was ruined. When I arrived, I smashed the tank to get him out, but it was too late. He had already overheated—and suffocated." As he spoke, the memory played out in his mind vividly, and Barnabas could see the truth of it.

"That's how you'd do it, I guess." Barnabas scratched his head.

The captain gave him a look. "Which is why the Jotuns have a very large number of backups and safety measures in their suits."

Barnabas paused. "So you're suggesting..."

"The person who did this knew a lot about the suits in general, and probably knew a lot about *his* suit in particular," Kelnamon said flatly. "They chose a time when Captain Ferqar—his friend—was out—"

"Tell me about the friend," Barnabas interrupted. A conveniently-absent bunkmate was an interesting detail.

"Another ship's captain," the captain explained. He shrugged. "Nothing particularly noteworthy about him. Well, I guess the fact that they were traveling with us in the first place. But it happens."

"*Another* ship's captain, as in, you're saying that the murdered Jotun was *also* a ship's captain?"

"Something in the navy." The Brakalon shrugged. "I don't know what, though. We sent a message to report it to them, and no one has come to check. We got word from someone in the government that they had received the message, and then...nothing." Kelnamon looked at Barnabas. "You said there were more destroyed ships. Was that one of them?"

"A Jotun ship was destroyed," Barnabas said neutrally.

"Great. So no one's coming to help."

I'm here, Barnabas commented to Shinigami, somewhat nettled.

We. We're here. Don't be so self-important.

Are you taking up murder investigations now?

Might as well. I'd make a good detective. The captain's been pretty honest with you, by the way—that is, assuming Brakalons have the same tells as humans for lying. No increased heart rate, sweating, or other signs of stress. His eyes don't shift suddenly to one side when he speaks.

Research whether those are tells for Brakalons, Barnabas told her. *I won't need them, but they'll be useful for Gar and Tafa.*

The captain barely noticed the small pause in their conversation. "And no one else will be coming because those other ships were supposed to handle it and they haven't reported back," Kelnamon said tonelessly.

"Yes." Barnabas considered this. "Therefore, I will be happy to investigate the murder and apprehend the killer. I will even be happy to bring them back to the proper jurisdiction." When the captain looked at him warily, Barnabas shrugged. "You're floating here with a shipload of fractious passengers and dwindling supplies, losing paying time, and you've got a murderer on the loose."

The captain gulped and nodded. "Right. I'll, uh—right. Given the circumstances, I think it would be possible to turn this investigation over to you."

"Good." It was convenient, especially since Barnabas had intended to investigate the murder whether the captain said yes or no.

Heads up, Shinigami reported, *someone is trying to get onto our ship.*

Species?

Not sure. And without knowing that, it's hard to determine gender, either.

Hmm. You have footage of them?

Yes.

File that away. I wouldn't rule out curiosity or simple panic at this point, but it's good to have a trail.

So...you're saying I can't zap them?

You can't zap them. And you can't use flamethrowers.

We officially know each other too well.

Agreed. Barnabas nodded to the captain, the exchange with Shinigami having taken only a split second. "Tell me everything you know."

"I don't know much," the captain admitted. "His friend hasn't said much. If you asked me, I'd say he had something to hide, but we have accounted for all his movements. We *did* check." He sounded defensive.

"Good," Barnabas said again. "I'll need a timeline of his movements from when he got on the ship, as well as the deceased's... What was his name, by the way?"

"Huword."

Barnabas nodded. "We'll start with your suspicions. Take me to Huword's traveling companion."

"Yes. Yes, of course." Kelnamon nodded, and his emotions were so strong that Barnabas did not even have to reach out to feel them.

The captain was terrified. Of what, Barnabas could not yet say. It could be nothing, he told himself as he followed Kelnamon from the room. With the Brakalon government ship destroyed, a murderer on board, and a strange authority taking over the case, Kelnamon had plenty of reasons to be worried.

But as his fears swirled, one thing was clear: Barnabas was at the center of them.

And why, Barnabas wondered, might that be?

CHAPTER FOUR

Before speaking to the dead captain's traveling companion, Barnabas detoured back to the *Shinigami* to call Jeltor.

He had a secondary motive as well: getting his crew back onto the ship now that he knew there was a murderer on the loose. He was worried that one of them would ask the wrong questions and get hurt.

He knew better than to tell any of them this, however. He had the sneaking suspicion that the first thing Gar and Shinigami would try to do would be to prove him wrong and go off asking questions.

Tafa, on the other hand, would probably be sensible about the whole thing. Barnabas enjoyed having someone on the ship who didn't have a death wish.

Shinigami connected the call while Barnabas sipped a glass of fruit juice. The ship was down to one of its last two cases, and he was beginning to get anxious about finishing their mission in time to go to High Tortuga and get more. Aebura, an Ubuara female who lived on the planet, had a secret recipe that Barnabas adored, and no matter how much the others teased him, he couldn't quite give up his addiction.

The screen cleared to show a Jotun. Which Jotun, Barnabas was not quite sure. He had begun to learn the vague feel of his acquaintances' thoughts and generally used that to identify individual Jotuns in person, but that wasn't a tactic he could use on a holocall.

"Jeltor?" He tapped the side of his screen as though it weren't working. "Video hasn't come online yet."

Liar.

Why are you watching?

I watch everything.

Luckily, no deception was necessary. "It's me," Jeltor said. The voice filtering from his suit was warm and pleasant.

"Oh, good. How are you?" Jeltor had been the subject of a trial for treason, the charges having been brought against him by corrupt senators. Although Jeltor had assured him that it would be fine, Barnabas had worried about leaving before the Senate had dropped the charges.

"I'm fine." Jeltor sounded amused now. "Are you going to call every few days like a—what was the phrase Shinigami used?—mother hen?"

Barnabas was opening his mouth to argue when he realized that the term suited him rather well. He cleared his throat self-consciously. "I don't see the problem with checking on my friends."

"It's much appreciated," Jeltor hastened to say. "On the other hand, don't you think you have more important things to worry about? I get the sense that fighting smugglers and corporations is a regular day-to-day thing for you." His body bobbed in a way that suggested emotion, and a moment later, he asked, "Speaking of which, did you find the ship making that distress call?"

"Unfortunately, that's my other reason for calling." Barnabas considered how best to approach this. "It's a Brakalon-registered civilian transport. Tell me, what do you know of a Captain Huword?"

"Huword?" Jeltor sounded surprised. "Great guy."

"So you know him," Barnabas confirmed with a sinking feeling in his gut.

"*Know* him? We went through the naval academy together." Jeltor chuckled. "You could say we were rivals, but really, we were good friends. We were just in the same ability class together, and we always tried to outdo one another. It wasn't just messing around, either. I think it kept us both sharp."

"Ability class." Barnabas frowned. The Jotun Naval captains controlled whole ships in the same way normal Jotuns controlled their bio-suits. "You mean, the same class of ships?"

"Yeah." Jeltor bobbed slightly. "Both of us tested up to frigate class. Not what we wanted, of course, but most people don't even make it into the academy to start with."

Barnabas nodded. The idea of trying to control the entire function of a warship with his mind was enough to give him a splitting headache. He gestured for Jeltor to keep talking. He did not want to tell the Jotun that his friend was dead. It was a bit cold, but he wanted, as much as possible, to get a good picture of the type of person Huword had been before Jeltor knew he was dead.

After all, people didn't get murdered for no reason, and the lack of other murders suggested that someone had targeted Huword specifically. Not because he'd interrupted another crime, for instance.

"There's not much more to say, I guess." Jeltor sounded nonplussed. "He was recently moved to the *Gar'aemon*. That might be something." Seeing Barnabas' confusion, he explained, "They moved him from one frigate to another. Huword was captain of the *Juteld*, which flies with the main bulk of the navy. We haven't been in a war in ages, so there wasn't much to do there, but it was in the center of everything. The *Gar'aemon* is a scout ship. It patrols the borders of our territory. A lot more to do, but possibly a demotion. No one was sure." He paused. "I hadn't had a chance to speak to him about it."

Barnabas leaned back in his chair and narrowed his eyes at the far wall, spinning a pen between his fingers as he thought. A possible demotion was an interesting detail, but he would think it more likely that the demoted captain would be the killer rather than the victim.

"What about Huword's other friends?" Asking about enemies might give Jeltor a suspicion of what was going on.

Jeltor considered this, and Barnabas wished he knew what the Jotun was thinking. "It's hard to think of anyone in particular," Jeltor said finally. "Gollwin, maybe? I haven't kept up with Huword lately so I couldn't tell you."

"But you remember him fondly."

"Oh, yes. I can't think of many who wouldn't. Just the usual assortment everyone builds up, romantic rivals and so on, and there weren't even many of those who didn't like Huword."

Barnabas tried not to get sidetracked by the idea of a Jotun romance. Would there be flowers of some kind? What kind of music did jellyfish listen to when they—

He'd been living with Shinigami for too long.

"Why are you asking?" Jeltor inquired now.

Barnabas steeled himself. "He was murdered." There was a long pause, during which the Jotun did not move. "Jeltor?"

"Murdered?" Jeltor repeated faintly.

Barnabas grimaced. "I'm afraid so. Hence the distress call."

"Why were they on a civilian transport?"

"I don't know." Barnabas shook his head. "I was hoping you could tell me. Shed some light on who Huword was, and why someone might want to kill him."

"It wasn't…some random thing, then." Jeltor was clearly agitated, the light bouncing off his trembling body as it floated in his suit.

Barnabas thought of the mysterious Jotun ship, and the network of satellites Shinigami had seen. "No. At this point, there's no chance. He was targeted. The killer knew the workings of Huword's suit and was blocking anyone from coming to investigate."

"What?"

"There was another ship waiting, and it had destroyed two ships who responded to the signal. It tried to take us out as well."

"You captured it, right?" Jeltor was pulsing now, something Barnabas assumed meant he was angry.

"We tried. They self-destructed. There's allegedly a Jotun government ship on the way, but they haven't shown up yet, and Shinigami hasn't seen them on the scanners. The Brakalon government ship was destroyed, as was a Shrillexian I assume had come to prey on the *Srisa* while it was stopped."

Jeltor thrashed slightly in the water. "Murdered," he repeated. "It isn't possible. It can't be! He was so young. He was my age!"

"I know." Barnabas realized he had no idea what Jeltor's age was. "I hoped you would tell me something that would make it obvious why he was killed, but it doesn't sound like he had any particular enemies."

"None who would do something like this!" Jeltor twisted and turned inside his suit's tank. "And who *would* do something like this? Why hold other ships away from the *Srisa* instead of just destroying it outright? It doesn't make sense. Who was running that ship?"

"A Jotun, we're fairly sure, but the ship was not of a make we'd ever seen before."

"Another *Jotun*?" Jeltor lapsed into a stream of cursing that did not particularly require translation—which was good since apparently a great deal of it was colloquial and wasn't translated by his implants. "I suppose that would make sense, although you told me that someone who understood the suits killed him."

Barnabas waited. As a friend, he wanted to reassure Jeltor right now. As someone invested in this case, however, he wanted to see what Jeltor would say. Shock was a powerful jolt to the system, and often it provided clarity, allowing someone to think of or reveal a fact they would not otherwise allow them-selves to see.

All Jeltor said, however, was, "You *must* solve this. Do you want me to come?"

"No, that's not necessary." Barnabas couldn't help laughing. "I was nervous enough leaving you there with the treason charges. I'm hardly going to take you away from that, only for you to wind up on a ship with an assassin who's killing Jotun ship's captains."

Jeltor managed a laugh as well, but it died quickly. "I mean it, Barnabas."

"I know you do," Barnabas hastened to assure him. "But give me some time to solve it on my own. I was only half-joking when I said this would be a dangerous place for you. Whoever came for him might come for you, too, and I'm not going to stand for that."

Jeltor said nothing, presumably lost in thought.

"He was traveling with a Captain Ferqar," Barnabas said. "Any knowledge of...him? Her? I'm sorry, I can't tell gender from your names yet."

"Why would you be able to tell that?" Jeltor asked, sounding mystified. "Do other species have names that vary from gender to gender?"

"Yes?"

"How confusing. We don't. Anyway, Ferqar also does border patrols. It makes sense that they would be traveling together—as much as any of this makes sense."

"Interesting. The captain of the *Srisa* said it seems like he's hiding something."

"He might be." Jeltor sounded grim now. "Who else would know everything about Huword?"

"He wasn't the one who killed him. His movements are all accounted for, I'm afraid. Whether he was an accomplice, though… That, I don't know."

Jeltor considered this. "Solve it," he said again. "You have to. Whoever would come for Huword—they're dangerous, Barnabas. It could be the Senate trying to get back at us for what we did with the Yennai Corporation."

Barnabas whistled. "You think it goes that high?"

"I don't know. Just be careful, and make sure the next one doesn't get a chance to use a self-destruct before you question them."

"Given that I'm on the ship in question," Barnabas said drily, "I will certainly strive to make sure of that."

CHAPTER FIVE

C aptain Ferqar was, in Barnabas' opinion, indistinguishable from any other Jotun except by the tenor of his thoughts. It was enough to make Barnabas wonder for a moment if there would be any way to prove, save by mind-reading, that Huword was the one who had died. Another Jotun would be able to see the deception, of course, but what if it only needed to be maintained for a brief time?

He chided himself for this ridiculous train of thought even as he probed the Jotun's thoughts. After all, nothing about this case seemed straightforward. He might as well search for the answers anywhere he could. There were plenty of memories Barnabas could find in which Ferqar was referred to by name, however, so he abandoned that theory with some relief.

He did not see any of the images he had found in Captain Kelnamon's memory, however, such as the smashed jar that he now realized was a Jotun biosuit tank.

He hadn't necessarily expected to. After all, Captain Kelnamon had said that Ferqar had a good alibi.

Still, when a Jotun naval captain was murdered in the middle of nowhere on a transport where no one else should know of him, his only acquaintance on board *was* the best suspect.

"Captain Ferqar." Barnabas smiled as he came into the room. "Thank you for speaking with me. Captain Kelnamon has allowed me to take over this case, and as the person on board who knew Captain Huword best, your help will be invaluable."

He held out a hand. The handshake was a common greeting among species, as it turned out, and with no worry of disease, Jotuns were always happy to shake their mechanical hands with anyone who wanted to do so. Ferqar shook Barnabas' now, and Barnabas detected wariness.

"Who, exactly, are you?" the Jotun asked him. "You're not Brakalon."

A real genius, this guy is. Shinigami was still sulking about being confined to the ship and had taken to commenting acerbically on anything and everything.

You know what he means, Barnabas said reprovingly. To Ferqar, he said, "I served as law enforcement in the Etheric Empire."

Ferqar experienced a spike of fear when Barnabas mentioned his past, but it came with no thoughts Barnabas could identify. He sometimes had trouble reading Jotuns' thoughts, but in this case, he was fairly certain there was no malice toward the Etheric Empire.

Barnabas waited. He wanted to test a hunch, and a

moment later, Ferqar had a sudden spike of thoughts: *the human who helped Captain Jeltor.*

"What is your name?" Ferqar asked. He sounded eager.

"Barnabas." Barnabas settled back in his chair and tried not to smile. Even through the garble of Jotun thoughts—he privately described it to Gar as listening to music through a bowl of jello—he could tell that Ferqar was not displeased to see him.

"I want to thank you," Ferqar said formally. "Unofficially, of course." There was a pause. "Is this off the record?"

"As long as it doesn't relate to the murder." Barnabas didn't let his expression change from a faint smile.

Another spike of fear, and then Ferqar's emotions swirled into such chaos that Barnabas could make neither heads nor tails of them. "It doesn't. I wanted to thank you for forcing the senators to stop treason proceedings against Captain Jeltor—and for defeating the Yennai Corporation."

There were so many emotions chasing each other through his head that Barnabas honestly could not tell if Ferqar was telling the truth.

"You weren't able to be at the battle, I'm guessing," he said as neutrally as he could.

"No. My route didn't allow it." He sounded bitter. Barnabas made a mental note of that.

"So, explain to me." Barnabas frowned. "Only a week or so ago, you were on a remote route that meant you could not join the battle against a massive fleet that had high odds of killing many of your colleagues. This, however, you boarded a fairly slow civilian transport with another captain who ran mostly the same routes—or was going to. How did that happen?"

Fear again, but there was the ring of truth in it when Ferqar said, bitterly amused, "I was giving him details of the routes someplace we could be away from listening ears." As the device in Barnabas' head translated, he noticed that the Jotun word for *ears* translated to *tentacles.* They must be all-sensory devices, but he could not tell how that would work. "Other Jotun ears, I mean," Ferqar continued. "Huword wanted to know what he'd gotten into."

"Oh?" In his years of playing "neutral" on Earth, Barnabas had learned to keep a conversation going without stating his position or impeding the flow of thoughts from the other person.

"If you know who we both are already, and it seems you do—" again, there was fear "—you should also know of Huword's...promotion." There was distaste in Ferqar's voice as well as a challenge.

"You mean, I'm guessing, the promotion that might or might not have been a promotion?" Barnabas lifted an eyebrow.

"Quite so." Ferqar sounded bitterly amused now. "Something I happen to know about."

There was genuine pain there, and Barnabas felt an unexpected stab of sympathy.

"Not a promotion for you, then, I'm guessing." He wished he could read the minutiae of Jotun posture and expressions.

"You guess correctly." Ferqar considered, and then said,

"The details aren't really important. If you're curious, I'm sure you can find the whole story."

He didn't seem to be hiding anything on that score, and Barnabas felt no urge to make him relive it. He knew what it felt like, after all, to want to avoid certain memories.

"You said Huword wanted to know what he was getting into, and you explained it all away from Jotun ears. Did he come to you, or did you go to him?"

Again, a swirl of emotion. "A little bit of both," Ferqar said neutrally. His mind was determinedly blank. Barnabas guessed it was likely a way to keep himself from saying something he didn't want to let slip.

But what *was* that? Barnabas sifted through recent memories and found nothing overtly incriminating, but everything seemed tinged with guilt and anger.

"Walk me through it," Barnabas requested now. The devil was in the details, as people said. Who knew what Ferqar might let slip?

Ferqar made a mechanical sound that Barnabas supposed was a sigh, but he didn't delay. "Several ships were called back to port after the...incident. The Yennai incident," he clarified when Barnabas frowned. Though Barnabas had trouble reading Jotun expressions, apparently they could read his just fine. "The Senate wanted to know everyone involved, how word had spread, if anyone had been pressured into joining you, or misled about the Senate being on board—that sort of thing. I think they assumed that because I wasn't involved, I was loyal to them."

"Which you're not," Barnabas said neutrally.

Ferqar froze. "This is a dangerous discussion."

"I can see how you'd think so, but do bear in mind that I was a part of that mission. As you mentioned, I helped Captain Jeltor." Barnabas settled back in his chair. "And I have no stake in Jotun politics. Well, not much of a one."

Ferqar paused. "I am loyal to the Jotun people and take my naval oaths very seriously." His voice was flat. "I was not contacted about the battle. When I was brought back, it was with a ship that could custom-Gate. They weren't... pleased. The Senate, I mean."

Barnabas sifted through this. He was guessing, at this point, that Ferqar's demotion and distance had precluded him from being a part of the battle, and the Jotun was not pleased about it.

But he couldn't be sure, not yet.

"In any case, I testified and then bumped into Huword. He knew the routes I ran, and we agreed to take a detour before our ships officially left port." Ferqar lifted a shoulder. "This was a round trip."

There was a flare of emotion and Barnabas frowned. They could verify the fact easily enough, which made Ferqar's evasiveness even more interesting.

"I see. So you two talked, and..."

"And?" Ferqar prompted, admirably playing Barnabas' own game.

Barnabas was better at it than Ferqar was, however. "I'm asking you," he replied equably.

"What do you want me to say?" Ferqar asked finally. "We weren't friends. We barely knew each other. This was the only connection we had—the breakdown of our careers." Again, a spike of emotion: grief and rage this time. "It was hardly something that inspired us to—"

Someone is coming your way, Shinigami broke in. Her voice was urgent.

Dangerous?

I think so. Someone came to the airlock door looking for you, then accessed the security feeds—I don't know who this is—then they set off for exactly where you are.

Barnabas made a split-second decision. "I'll be back." He stood, buttoning his suit jacket. "There's an urgent matter."

Ferqar settled into silence, and Barnabas sensed genuine annoyance. Ferqar's anger over his ruined career, at least, was genuine.

Barnabas paused. "I don't mean to dredge up uncomfortable memories," he said finally. "What happened to you —to you both—is something that happens across species, and it costs everyone when good people are not able to do their jobs."

After the sudden burst of emotion, Ferqar seemed to be keeping a tight rein on his feelings. His mechanical head nodded once. After a pause, Barnabas shook his head slightly and went into the corridor. He would have to untangle Ferqar's strange words later—

Something hit him *hard* on the back of the head.

Whether it was meant to be a killing blow, Barnabas couldn't say, but it was certainly meant to incapacitate him. He stumbled sideways into a wall and whirled to face his attacker.

Baggy clothing, half-structured with armor, covered a lanky frame that Barnabas could not quite identify, while a mask and hood obscured the shape of the face. There must be some technology he didn't see in it because there were no eye or mouth holes. It was like fighting a comic book character, which did *not* make him particularly happy.

Tabitha had spent weeks at one point trying to get him into comics. Barnabas had never confessed to her that the real reason he hated them wasn't the cartoonish violence or overblown characterization. It was the fact that he got far too drawn into the stories and was never going to know how many of them ended.

He still sometimes had dreams about the characters fighting alien species with him, a fact he hoped she would never find out.

His attacker, meanwhile, seemed deeply surprised that Barnabas was not in a heap on the floor. They recovered quickly, however. One foot punched up and out to drive Barnabas back, and again, the assassin struck with what should have been bone-crunching force. Barnabas felt his skin break, and blood burst from capillaries in the start of a brilliant bruise. Then the nanites went to work, healing the damage within seconds.

"And I thought I'd have to work to find you," he told the assassin with savage satisfaction. "But here you are."

The assassin waited warily, head cocked to the side, and Barnabas struggled to recognize any familiar line to the bone structure.

Shinigami, is there anything you can tell about the physiology here? What am I dealing with?

Possibly Torcellan—or possibly human, I guess. But very slim. Whatever species, probably a female since they're so small.

The assassin feinted, then danced away again when Barnabas reacted more quickly than she expected.

And *she's good*, Shinigami commented. *Very good. I haven't seen most of you lot hit that hard.*

Someone else must have come up with that technology. Barnabas thought he heard a faint mechanical hum. *I think there's an exosuit involved somehow. I'll try to get it off her. I need to take the mask off to know who she is, anyway—and this technology will let us know what we should be on the lookout for in the future.*

Without warning, the assassin launched herself straight up, dislodging a ceiling plate and disappearing into the duct system.

Shinigami! Barnabas took two steps and leaped as well. He grabbed the edge of one panel and had just enough time to see the assassin looking straight down at him before the panel was slammed back into place on his fingertips.

Normally, he would have been able to hold on, but the sheer force of it caused the nerves and joints to fail, and Barnabas fell back into the hallway, shocked. The assassin had gotten away.

Can you—do you have any eyes—

No. Shinigami sounded sober suddenly. *Are you all right?*

Just get it out of the way. Barnabas stood up and flexed his fingers. He watched them heal.

...What?

Whatever your joke is about me losing my grip and falling. He seemed to have absorbed Ferqar's bad mood. *Just say it and get it out of the way.*

There was silence as he walked.

Well?

I've seen you fight, you know. She still sounded sober. *I know how hard you must have gotten hit. You don't just give up.*

If you ask me, they ran because they knew that fight wasn't a sure thing.

She vanished from his mind and Barnabas stopped, frowning. Once, Shinigami would just have teased him. As they got closer, she might have been offended that he hadn't believed in her.

But this—the quiet concern and support—was new.

"Every time I think I have her figured out…" he muttered as he started back down the corridor. He shook his head slightly, and a smile played on his lips.

Back in the interrogation room, Ferqar was waiting quietly. His mechanical head looked around as Barnabas entered, and Barnabas could see the jellyfish-like body in the tank swivel as well. He wondered how much Ferqar saw with his real body versus with the biosuit, and made a mental note to ask Shinigami about it when she was in a better mood.

"I'm sorry for the interruption," he said smoothly, sitting down once more. His fingers still ached, and he held them out of sight to keep Ferqar from noticing the still-healing injury. The nanites were quick, but with the bones *completely* crushed, they had a lot to do.

Ferqar said nothing. He had sunk into silence.

"Who do *you* think killed Huword?" Barnabas asked bluntly.

He was trying to provoke a reaction, and he got one. Fear spiked through Ferqar. Inside its tank, the body pulsed.

When Ferqar spoke, however, his voice was flat. "Someone he wronged."

Barnabas raised his eyebrows. "An interesting response." He had been attacked by the female he assumed was the assassin—someone who wanted him dead, in any case—but he couldn't rule out Ferqar's being involved just yet.

"Is it?" Ferqar sounded a bit angrier now. "Is it 'interesting' to you? I've had a lot of time to think about it, in case you don't remember—about the fact that someone on board can get through biosuits. It isn't possible for that to happen by accident. A human can get killed in a bar fight, just like a Torcellan or a Shrillexian. Even a Brakalon can get hit hard enough or stabbed or shot. But Jotun biosuits are made to withstand all of that. A punch, a kick—even normal ammunition isn't going to breach a suit. Someone *wanted* to kill him. And they planned it."

Barnabas blinked. Ferqar's reasoning was good, he had to admit, and when he mentioned someone on board who could get through biosuits, his fear had been genuine. There were still no images in his head of whatever had happened to Huword, but the speculation and terror of death rang true.

There was guilt there too, but Barnabas knew from experience that many survivors carried guilt with them. In this case, Ferqar hadn't been there when the assassin struck. He would feel guilty that he hadn't helped his acquaintance, relieved that he hadn't also been killed…and even more guilty that he was relieved.

As much as Barnabas didn't want this case to become

more complicated, he had to admit that it didn't look like Ferqar had been involved. He nodded slightly.

"That perspective is useful," he said as gently as he could. "For another species, we would think it *might* be a crime of passion, something done impulsively. It wouldn't have occurred to me that it *couldn't* be just an argument that got out of hand. You've helped me get closer to the truth, Ferqar, and I will keep you safe. You have nothing to fear."

"I know I have nothing to fear," Ferqar said sharply. "If they wanted me dead, I'd be dead. That much is obvious, isn't it?"

Again, there was a true fear. He'd had a great deal of time to ponder this, Barnabas thought, while he was shut up here on a stopped transport with his traveling companion dead.

Barnabas nodded slightly.

"I know he was only an acquaintance," he said quietly, "but I am sorry for your loss."

There was no response from Ferqar, only bitterness, and after a moment, Barnabas left.

CHAPTER SIX

Barnabas rubbed the back of his head as he made his way to the airlock where the *Shinigami* was latched onto the *Srisa*.

Shinigami.

Yes?

What do we think the odds are that Kelnamon was involved?

What? Are you serious?

It's the only thing that makes sense. In the area outside the airlock, Barnabas looked around. Whoever had tried to get in here before, they didn't seem to be around now. The whole ship was very, very quiet.

He didn't like it.

Shinigami, having seen him, opened the door and he went inside, still turning the incident over and over in his head. If the ship was so quiet...

He's the only one aside from Ferqar who even knows I'm on board for this purpose.

"You're on board, remember?" The voice emerged from

Shinigami's body as she maneuvered it painstakingly around a corner. "You can speak aloud."

"Force of habit." Barnabas managed a small smile as she walked jerkily towards him.

"Seriously, how do you do this?" Shinigami asked, sounding annoyed. "Only one set of eyes? Can't see behind you? Navigating is insane. And you're supposed to watch where you're walking *and* watch where you're putting your feet? How do you do it?"

"Proprioception, mainly." Barnabas pretended to study the wall so that she wouldn't feel self-conscious. "We don't need to look at our bodies as they move because we develop an idea of where they are in space. It's why toddlers look at their hands and feet while they move and adults don't. As you get better at this, you'll acquire the same sense."

"Hmph."

"Part of why you're struggling is that we haven't done this before, you know." Barnabas looked at her now. She had almost reached him. "You could write some of the programming so that when other AIs receive bodies, they'll know how to use them better."

"Nuh-uh. If I must suffer, so must they."

"That is *not* the spirit in which this ship and crew operate."

She stuck her tongue out at him in response. "So, Captain Kelnamon. Tell me your theory. Distract me."

"Well, he's incredibly well-placed to have done it," Barnabas began. "He has the codes for each room, could override security footage, and could get an assassin on-board—and then off."

Shinigami stopped suddenly. "You think the ship we encountered when we first got here..."

"Was the assassin?" Barnabas shrugged. "You tell me. It makes sense, though, doesn't it?"

Shinigami whistled—or, more accurately, tried to whistle. She pursed her lips...and very clearly whistled from one of the speakers on the wall. Barnabas gave a laugh he hastily turned into a cough.

"Just use your internal speaker."

"I couldn't find the— Not important." She folded her arms. "Keep walking, funny man. Explain the distress signal to me. Because it seems to me that someone who was careful enough to sneak on board and plan an assassination was probably observant enough to see you arrive, speak with Kelnamon, and then go speak with Ferqar. It wouldn't take a genius to figure out why you were there."

"That's a weak part of the theory," Barnabas admitted. "Both of those things. In terms of the distress signal, I don't see why he had to observe protocol on that. I don't know how commonly known it is that Brakalon law requires him to stop. Even if it *is* common knowledge, would any of his Brakalon passengers mind if, instead of trapping them in the middle of nowhere with a murderer, he kept going to port and just pretended he would speak to authorities there? Would the authorities care?"

Shinigami considered this. "You're growing as a person, you know. There was a time when it wouldn't even have occurred to you to ask whether the law was commonly followed."

Barnabas gave a small smile, but he couldn't really enjoy the humor of the moment. None of the pieces of this fit together in his head. He was used to knowing who his enemy was. In this case, he knew almost nothing. The people best placed to pull this off, it seemed, had not been involved.

"Anyway," Shinigami continued, "if we're going down the rabbit hole, the law might not even be what he said it is."

Barnabas stopped dead. "Then why stop and broadcast a signal?"

"I don't know." She shrugged, although she didn't expend the energy to turn around and shrug *at* him. Instead, she continued walking grimly, determined to make it to the end of the hallway.

He could understand her determination. Practicing a new skill wasn't always pleasant. "You're right; we *are* going down the rabbit hole." He considered. "If you can get us video from the bridge and confirm that Kelnamon was the one who turned the distress signal on and that he did it without prompting from the rest of the crew or passengers, we can eliminate that as a... Wait, why aren't you just looking up Brakalon legal codes?"

"I tried, and they're unreadable. I swear the whole thing is a metaphor. I'm still trying to parse whether this one section is referring to improvised explosives or jaywalking. What's that expression on your face?"

"Trying to imagine what possible language could encompass both of those things."

Shinigami snickered. "I'll research Kelnamon's movements. I have to say, though, I don't think the captain is behind this. He had no motive."

"That *you* know of."

"I suppose."

Barnabas rubbed the back of his head again. *"Damn, they hit me hard."*

"You're still healing from that?" She sounded genuinely concerned.

"A little bit. Mostly cleanup from the bruise. That's a process. The cracked bones are easier to fix."

"All right, that does it, if they managed to crack *your* thick skull, there's something shady going on here. I have to go research something." Shinigami hobbled over to a doorway and de-animated the body so that it slumped face-first into the alcove.

"Shinigami?"

"Yes?"

"Was that an insult or a statement of fact?"

"Yes."

Barnabas rolled his eyes and went off to get a glass of juice.

In the kitchen, he found Tafa eating a bowl of something that looked like sawdust. She had gone off with Gar at their last stop to resupply and had told everyone that she finally had the ingredients to make one of her favorite dishes. Barnabas now found himself hoping she wouldn't offer him any of it.

"So, what's going on with the murder case?" she asked around a mouthful of food.

Barnabas hid a grimace. He was a stickler for table manners, but both Tabitha and Shinigami had informed him that he was not allowed to mention people's manners to them since it was insufferably pretentious—or in Tabitha's somewhat more flowery language, "douche-canoe-y."

He distracted himself by pouring a glass of juice. "I interviewed Captain Huword's traveling companion—briefly—then got attacked, so, unfortunately, I have more questions now than I started with, not less."

"You were attacked?" Tafa sounded surprised. "Then how is this still a case? The person who attacked you *must* be the murderer, right?"

"It's likely, but unfortunately, I wasn't able to apprehend her." Barnabas *did* allow himself a grimace at that. He steeled himself and joined Tafa at the table.

"What? She *beat* you?" She looked genuinely flabbergasted.

"It happens, you know," Barnabas snapped tetchily.

"Not often. Gar said you once took on hundreds of mercenaries."

"The stories are somewhat overblown, and overwhelming numbers do not help in the case of… Not important."

"No, seriously, I wanna see the fight." Tafa looked around. "Shinigami, did you holo it?"

"Yes," Shinigami's voice announced.

Barnabas dropped his face into his hands. "Do we have to do this?"

"Yes," they said in unison.

"Hey," Gar said, entering the kitchen.

"Oh, good. Let's have everyone see it." Barnabas drained

his glass in one bitter gulp. "Why don't we invite Captain Kelnamon as well?"

"Eh?" Gar looked at Tafa.

"Don't listen to him." She waved her spoon, having gotten past the phase of being awed by Barnabas. "He fought the murderer, and he *lost*. We're watching the video for clues."

"Oh, for *clues*?" Barnabas looked up. "That's less embarrassing."

Everyone scooched their chairs over to a nearby holo-screen and watched the fight unfold. Barnabas emerged from the door of Captain Ferqar's quarters, only to be hit in the back of the head by the masked opponent.

The fight, such as it was, seemed even quicker than it had at the time. Barnabas sighed and settled back in his chair, although he winced when he saw himself drop from the ceiling.

"What happened there?" Tafa asked Barnabas.

"She smashed the ceiling panel down on the tips of my fingers." Barnabas curled his hands into protective fists, burying his nails in his palms. "It crushed the bones."

Tafa and Gar gaped at him.

"Very unpleasant," Barnabas said shortly. "Although... very effective."

Gar looked back at the screen with a queasy expression. He was still watching, along with Barnabas, when Tafa said loudly, "*Ha!*"

Gar jumped. "Er, yes?"

"She's not biological," Tafa announced.

"*What?*" Barnabas demanded at the same time as Shinigami said, "How did *you* know that?"

"Whoa, wait, back up." Barnabas stood up and looked accusingly at the speakers. "*You* knew?"

"Yes. Well, I suspected it."

"Why didn't you tell me?"

"I was trying to confirm it before I said anything!" Shinigami flickered into being in full armor, perched on top of a cabinet by the holoscreen. She tilted her head curiously at Tafa. "How *did* you know, though?"

"Something about the movements." Tafa shrugged. "And the head is a weird shape, so there's that. What are the odds that some random new kind of alien showed up just to commit murder on a civilian ship?"

Barnabas nodded, bemused.

"And something about the way the joints function just doesn't seem right," Tafa added. She pointed at the screen. "But the kicker is, look at the way it jumps up into the ceiling there."

Shinigami obligingly slowed the video down.

"There's no real muscle engagement," Tafa pointed out. "In any other bipedal species, we'd see the tension in the torso. There's none here. It's subtle, but it's definitely different."

Barnabas frowned at the screen. "Shinigami? What gave it away to *you*?"

"The fact that she—well, if it's a she—hit you hard enough to dent your skull," Shinigami said. "I was surprised she'd slammed the panel down so hard, too, but that first hit was what sealed the deal. There was no weapon, but she hit you incredibly hard at an angle that would be difficult to generate the power for using an organic muscle structure. So I started looking, and I realized that the pocket of space above that panel was pretty small. So not only did she generate an extraordinary amount of force on that one panel dropping down, but she *also* got away without any place for a roughly human-sized alien to fit. Which means..." She gave Barnabas a meaningful look.

"She's still there!" He was on his feet. "Gar, come on."

"No, no, no." Shinigami's voice stopped him. She sighed. "She *disassembled* herself."

Barnabas froze and looked slowly over his shoulder. "You are *kidding* me."

"I'm not. Furthermore, I think *she* was the person trying to get in here before, and I saw her greet someone in the hallway as they passed, which suggests she bought passage. There's an explanation that starts to link up with some of the rest of what we know, too."

"Which is?" Barnabas frowned up at her.

Shinigami took her time before answering, and when she did, she sounded exceedingly pleased with herself.

"It's a Jotun."

CHAPTER SEVEN

"We have to do this logically," Barnabas said. He was pacing around the armory dressed in his armor. "She's easily capable of fighting me, and I have a ship full of civilians to protect. Ideas?"

"The first thing is to make sure she doesn't have any allies," Shinigami suggested reasonably. She was in her artificial body, swinging her arms in an approximation of Barnabas' warmup exercises. "You suspected Kelnamon and Ferqar."

"I think we can now expand that to include any other Jotun on the ship," Barnabas said.

"The only other *registered* one is Ferqar," Shinigami said. "And clearly it wasn't him."

"Are you sure? A Jotun naval captain can pilot an entire ship. Why couldn't they pilot a suit remotely?"

"Well, for one thing, that mechanism is biomechanical. None of it is ever done remotely."

Barnabas chewed his lip. "Hrmph."

"Which isn't to say that it *couldn't* work that way," Shinigami continued, "but I am almost one hundred percent certain that she was the one who came to look at the airlock door the other day, which means I got a scan then, and there was definitely Jotun biomatter in a sufficient amounts for this to be another Jotun."

"Okay." Barnabas rubbed his face. "So we can't tell Kelnamon just to get all the Jotun passengers in one place. He has to be in on it, doesn't he?"

"Not necessarily," Tafa opined. She was sitting on a stack of mats at one side of the room, swinging her legs. Her blue skin glowed faintly in the dim lights. "With this many berths on the ship, he probably doesn't see everyone who gets one, and it's not a ship that's going to make the passengers go through a bioscanner to board."

"Interplanetary security sounds like a nightmare," Barnabas muttered.

"It is, actually." Gar looked over from where he, too, was putting on his armor. "The measures taken on Devon—I'm sorry, *High Tortuga*—aren't available to most planetary governments. That means they can't *really* stop someone from setting down on their planet. There will always be enough of a gap in the air defenses for something to slip through. Meanwhile, there are so many pilots ready to make a quick buck, and so many who don't even care, that a person can usually get wherever they want to without having anyone bother them. If they have money, of course, and this one clearly does."

Barnabas sighed heavily.

"How do you know she's rich?" Tafa challenged Gar.

"Easy. They have a custom biosuit that works extremely well in hand-to-hand combat, and a very good ship and accomplice."

"The other Jotun," Barnabas said neutrally.

"Well, yeah." Gar looked at him, bemused. "They were working together, right?"

"How do you know that?"

"I mean, I— Well, I just *do*. I mean, I don't. It makes sense, though, right?" He scratched his head. "Shinigami, back me up."

"I'm afraid I can't." Shinigami's voice was regretful although her face was blank. "With technology like this, I see no reason the pilot of that ship couldn't have gotten the assassin off the *Srisa* pretty much immediately if they were working together. If they didn't collaborate to do that, therefore, it means—well, either they *weren't* working together, or the two of them were waiting for someone specific. Which was almost certainly *not* us."

Barnabas nodded slowly. His sense of self-preservation had flared up as soon as Shinigami said, "Someone specific," but he knew the assassin could not have predicted that *he'd* be the one to get there.

"You're *sure* someone was piloting the ship that blew up," he said.

"Yes. I *did* scan it. I wasn't able to get specific readings since I couldn't hook into their systems, but I know there was someone there."

"None of this makes sense!" Barnabas waved his arms for emphasis.

"At least we agree on something," Gar said helpfully. "If

they were working together and waiting for someone—that makes sense, Shinigami, thank you—then it was probably the Jotun government, right?"

Barnabas stopped, a chill going through him. "You might be onto something," he said slowly.

Everyone looked at him.

"Jeltor said he wondered if this was retaliation for what happened with the Yennai fleet," Barnabas explained. "Now, *Ferqar* may not have been involved, but Jeltor seemed to think Huword *was*. So the question is, *was* this a Jotun government assassination?"

"The level of sophistication would make sense in that case," Shinigami said after a moment. "Both in the ship and the assassin's biosuit. It's stuff we haven't seen before. Where better for it to come from than some deep dark government lab?"

"Says the government lab project."

"Listen here—"

"Yeah, yeah." Barnabas waved a hand. "What's weird to me, in that case, is that the assassin, who has the capabilities to overpower most other aliens, *and* has extremely good tech backup, wouldn't just disable a distress signal. Is the ship wired that well?"

"No," Shinigami said promptly. "They wouldn't even have had to go to the bridge to disable both that and outbound communications beyond repair."

"Ugh." Gar sounded glum now. "So it *doesn't* make sense that they're working together. I *do not* get this."

"Okay, so they're not working together." Barnabas snapped his fingers. "This assassin took out Huword, and the person on the ship was trying to keep everyone else away until…someone specific could get there to apprehend them?"

Gar was clutching his head. "This keeps going around in circles."

"But we're getting closer," Barnabas said. He gave a somewhat manic grin.

"Unless you're going in exactly the opposite direction," Shinigami pointed out.

"That's enough from you. Look at what you're doing to poor Gar. Tafa, any observations?"

"Nope." Tafa shook her head. "I'm all out. My whole contribution was noticing the biosuit."

"Still helpful." Barnabas nodded decisively. "All right, here's my plan. We assume Kelnamon isn't involved. It's in the best interests of the assassin to make sure no one notices, right? No, we can't even assume that. *Fuck*. I got nothin'. Shinigami, do you have any idea where the Jotun is right now?"

"No."

"Can you lock down the ship so that people are at least held in small groups?"

"Yes."

"Do that, then." Barnabas looked at Gar. "Looks like you and I are going door to door until we find this thing. Hopefully, it's not still in the damned walls."

"I'm coming with you," Shinigami announced. Her body appeared in the doorway. "And before you say no, remember that I have scanners built into this body. If the Jotun *is* in the walls, I'm the best chance you have of finding them."

Barnabas sighed. "I can also sense their minds, you

know. Did you remember that?"

"I...did not." She sounded a bit prickly. "But with so many people around, and only a fleeting impression of them before, I think we should both go."

"No."

"You've just locked them, whoever they are, in a small area with some civilians. Do you really want to take the chance of them starting to take hostages?"

Barnabas groaned. "All right, you can come along, but let the record show that I have a bad feeling about this."

Shinigami, Barnabas said a few minutes later as the three of them strode down the empty halls, *tell Captain Kelnamon that we know who the murderer is and that we'll be searching the ship room by room. Then see if he tries to do anything shady.*

Evil, Gar commented.

Agreed. Shinigami flashed a smile. It showed up about a second later than it would normally have, but she was starting to get the hang of emoting with the body. A few seconds later, she reported, *He thanked me, and he's just sitting there drumming his fingers on the desk. Now he's typing. Looking at the screen... No, wait, I can just go into the computers...*

There was a pause. Barnabas stopped briefly, thinking he heard something nearby, but no more sounds came and he continued.

He's started to write a briefing, Shinigami said finally. *It's to the Brakalon government and describes you taking over. He says he turned the investigation over to you because of what you said about the destroyed ship and says you've solved the murder. He's typing who it is...*

All three of them looked at one another, eyes wide. If Kelnamon was typing everything out, that meant he already knew.

Wait, never mind. Shinigami sounded grumpy. *He stopped. He was just prepping it, I guess. He's telling some of the crew to ready the engines and a holding cell. Oh, now he's asking if it's one of the crew, and what size holding cell he needs.*

Tell him to wait for everything. Whether or not it's one of the crew—which I doubt—I don't want them wandering around the halls.

Okay, I'll— What was that?

All three of them, their senses enhanced well beyond normal levels, looked sharply up as they came into the main living area of the ship. The kitchen lay in a three-story space decorated with plants. It was probably designed to keep people from going crazy during their weeks of travel in a metal box hurtling through space. Other levels opened onto this room as well, and metal catwalks ran around the sides of it on the other two levels.

Nothing moved in the shadows.

There's someone up there, Shinigami said simply. *I'm scanning, but they must know we're able to do that now. They're— wait, I got it—there's some material blocking me from scanning biomatter, but I got a glimpse. Our Jotun is up there.*

Go!

Barnabas took a running leap and swung up onto the

first level of catwalks. He heard Gar take off behind him, and Shinigami gave a whoop as she, too, jumped for the catwalk.

There was a thud, and Barnabas sincerely wished he could look. He couldn't take even a moment to stop scanning the area for the Jotun assassin, however, and even if he knew where the person was, he didn't trust Shinigami not to kill him if he laughed at her.

Safer not to look.

He landed lightly on the catwalk and spun to scan the space.

Above him, someone burst into a sprint. Barnabas looked up and saw someone in a long cloak. *Shinigami, you were right about the signal-blocking material.* He hopped onto the railing and leaped to pull himself up to the third level.

The Jotun assassin looked over her shoulder and saw him. She paused for a split-second. Barnabas had just enough time to picture her smashing his fingers again before she took off, heading for the door that led into the corridors of the third level.

He gave chase. "Stop right there!"

I must ask...does that ever *work?*

You're just grumpy because you fell. He could hear Gar laughing internally as well, probably at both, and for a moment, Barnabas felt *happy.* He couldn't remember the last time he'd felt such a pleasant, uncomplicated emotion.

He liked doing this job with a team, it turned out.

He was still smiling as he rounded the corner into the darkened hallway and ran straight into a punch. The Jotun's fist shot out with devastating speed. It should have broken Barnabas' ribs, if not made a hole into his chest cavity, but he had armor his opponent wasn't expecting. It had driven out all the breath from his lungs in a surprised whoosh, though. The Jotun staggered back, jerky movements betraying her shock.

Gar's footsteps were close behind, so the Jotun took off again, having failed to kill Barnabas for the second time.

"Get down!" Gar yelled, and he hurtled over Barnabas and took off at high speed after the assassin.

Get moving, Vigilante!

Can't—breathe—

You should be saying fifty Hail Jeans as a thank you to the universe for letting you survive that punch.

Barnabas tried to picture any of the monks he'd known praying to Jean Dukes and had to fight with everything he had not to lose his breath a second time in hysterical laughter. He took three loping steps, trying to spur his body back into breathing properly by forcing it to use breath and then pushed himself into a sprint once more.

Barnabas, I think she's going for the shuttles! Gar's mental tone was panicked. *I'll do what I can to catch her, but—*

A shot rang out, and there was a yell of pain.

Gar! Barnabas put on a burst of speed and swung around a corner as fast as he could. Gar was slumped against a railing, one hand clamped over the other arm. The assassin looked over her shoulder and kept running.

"Stop!" Barnabas yelled. He took his chance to leap over Gar and ran for all he was worth.

The Jotun's biosuit, however, was *fast.* She disappeared into the shuttle bay and turned, holding one mechanical hand to an electronics panel.

Shinigami!

Fuck fuck fuck fuck!

The door slammed down.

Fuck fuck fuck fuck fuck! Keep running. I'm trying to open it!

Barnabas closed the distance at top speed. *Shinigami!*

Making progress, keep going. Fuck fuck fuck, almost there, don't stop. WAIT, ABSOLUTELY DO STOP!

Barnabas ran into the door at top speed and bounced. From behind the closed door, he heard the alarms that accompanied the airlock.

So I'm guessing that's a no-go on overriding the programs.

Not even the airlock. She shorted a bunch of it and left systems in place to make it look like things were functioning. By the way, even though we were basing it off bad information the first time, I think we were right—that's a female.

How can you tell? More importantly, get a trace on that damned ship!

Already done. Come back to the ship, and we'll get going. Err...when you can walk. Gar's fine, but not fine enough to carry you.

Barnabas groaned and rolled over. *I think I broke my nose.*

Oooh, let it heal crooked. It'll give your face some character.

Barnabas rolled his eyes as he pushed himself up and hobbled back to where Gar, too, had managed to stand. *Goddammit, I hate it when they run.*

Think of it this way—there are no civilians in the way anymore.

I do like that. Barnabas looked at where the nanites had already healed the bullet wound. They hobbled back to the main living area. *Shinigami?*

Yes?

I don't want to drop down three flights. For the love of God, find me a staircase.

CHAPTER EIGHT

K antar settled into her seat as the shuttle powered
away into the darkness. Normally, she wouldn't
trust her odds against a ship like the *Shinigami*, but she
knew she could get a reasonable head start while their
crew got back to the ship.

Not only that, she'd paid an exorbitant amount to have
crates loaded at the beginning of the *Srisa's* run on a later
stop. With those materials, she had managed to significantly upgrade the shuttle, as well as install several types of
decoys that would allow her to lose any pursuers.

Hopefully. The *Shinigami* had already launched tracing
measures, and Kantar had to hope she could disable them
soon.

She bobbed in the warm water of her tank and tried to
release her anxiety, but she could not. She had become one
of the best assassins in this sector, stronger than any
organic life form, and so at home in her biosuit that she
never took it off.

Kantar resented the biosuits. The Jotuns' unique physiology allowed them certain opportunities in the form of controlling a great deal of machinery with their minds. Other species, it seemed, could not do so on the same scale.

But other species could walk on their own. They could use hands and arms to manipulate tools, while Jotuns were forced to use suits to do the same. If enough other species had developed in water perhaps the Jotuns would not be the odd ones out, but as it was...

Speculation was pointless. Kantar had spent most of her life fine-tuning and learning to use her suit until she could engage in hand-to-hand combat the way any other species could. It wasn't the typically clunky gadget-dependent Jotun fighting with flamethrowers or built-in knives and guns. No. Kantar could strike with her hands and feet, use an opponent's physiology to throw or pin them, and manipulate machinery so that no one noticed she was Jotun unless they saw the metal of the suit.

Sometimes it occurred to her that, through her struggle, she had become better at combat than most people could *ever* hope to be. She wanted to take joy in that, but she was still angry. If she had been born anything other than Jotun, her life would have been very different.

She looked up sharply when one of her sensors beeped. The *Shinigami* was powering up and getting ready to pursue her.

She switched on the cloaking algorithms. The upgrade she had installed on the shuttle used three different generators, all of which cycled through different cloaking mechanisms at unpredictable intervals. Kantar used it on her ship, and she had thought it was unbreakable.

That was before she knew she was being pursued by the *Shinigami*, however.

She felt a stab of fear. Had the Jotun Senate sent Barnabas after her? He wouldn't be helping them, surely. Of course, he wouldn't be the first one they had turned.

She had to find safety, and she had to find it *now*. She accelerated the shuttle to top speed, settled back in her seat, and tried to remain calm.

"She's engaged—oh, that's interesting." Shinigami sat down in the seat next to Barnabas. Only the final movement was somewhat graceless.

"What's interesting?" Barnabas looked over.

"She's using a very intriguing method of cloaking. Expensive to produce, most likely."

"She's a Jotun with an extremely good custom-made suit who can fight like an organic life form. I don't see why we'd be surprised to run across an expensive cloaking system."

"I'm not *surprised*; it's just interesting." Shinigami crossed one leg over the other. "And to answer the question I know you're going to ask—yes, I can crack it. Between our peek into the Jotun fleet and our run-in with the Yennai Corporation, I'm up to date on every form of cloaking this sector has to offer."

Barnabas gave a small smile. "I *was* going to ask that, you're right. As a follow-up—"

"You want me to cloak us so she can't see us, send a decoy so that she thinks we've gone in another direction, and follow her on the sly?"

"Yes."

"Already done."

"Remind me to give you a raise. How does one pay an AI?"

"When that AI just got a body? In *shoes*."

"I should have seen that coming." Barnabas heaved a sigh and stood, walking toward the door. "I'll ask Bethany Anne for recommendations."

"Ask her about bags, too."

"Bags? Like…purses?"

"Yes."

"What are you going to keep in a purse?"

Shinigami looked at him like he was absolutely insane. "*Guns.*"

Barnabas shook his head and left.

"Where are you going?"

"To talk to Jeltor. You seem to have everything under control, after all."

"So I'm in command?" Shinigami called over her shoulder as the doors closed. "Barnabas? Am I in command?" *Barnabas?*

Barnabas sighed. *No, you are* not *in command.*

Then I'm going to the armory. And before you argue, remember that I can watch the bridge just fine from anywhere.

Why are you going to the armory? Why are we talking this way?

Force of habit, as you said. And I'm going to train. Shinigami's usual careless tone slipped away for a moment. *What she could do with her biosuit was impressive.*

It was, wasn't it? Barnabas smiled. He approved of taking inspiration from opponents. *Enjoy.*

I think that's overly optimistic, but I'll practice.

Barnabas whistled as he made his way down the hallway to his rooms. When he slid into his chair and began the call to Jeltor, however, his face fell. He didn't have good news to report.

When the image came up on the screen this time, Barnabas' eyes strayed to the left side of the suit, where he'd noticed a telltale scratch when speaking to Jeltor previously. It was there, and he felt a small wave of satisfaction. He didn't know why this hadn't occurred to him before.

"Hello, Jeltor."

"You didn't find anything," Jeltor guessed. He bobbed in the water listlessly.

"Not exactly." Barnabas cleared his throat and considered what to say. He'd spent so many decades choosing his words carefully that it was second nature at this point to pause before he spoke. "We found the assassin and are pursuing her."

"What?" Jeltor became much more animated.

Barnabas realized he could tell the strength of Jeltor's emotions, if not the exact nature thereof.

"You're *pursuing* her?" Jeltor continued. "How did she get away from you? I've seen you fight—"

"Oh, trust me, I'll be hearing about this from Shinigami for quite a long time." Barnabas was trying to cheer Jeltor up, and he was happy to hear what sounded like a chuckle. "The thing is—and this is a bit awkward—the assassin was Jotun."

"I should have known." Jeltor sounded angry. "I should have known when you told me how the murder was done. I think I *did* know, and I just..." His voice trailed away, and there was real grief there. "Can you imagine how horrifying it must have been?" he asked finally, and Barnabas saw that Jeltor was trying to explain. "To die slowly, to know that you couldn't stop it. He was completely helpless."

Barnabas could find no words for this.

The truth was, he *did* know, although it was not on his account. It was Catherine who had taught him the agony of helplessness as she had wasted away while he had prayed with all his heart for her to survive, no matter what the cost.

Of course, he had believed *he* would be the one to bear the cost.

"Yes," was all he said now, very quietly. "I can imagine."

Whatever Jeltor heard in his voice, he was surprised into silence for a moment.

Finally, Jeltor said, "It would have had to be a Jotun. I should have warned you. Only a Jotun would know to do the things they did. But I hoped—I thought that no Jotun would do something like that. It was so cruel."

Barnabas shook his head slightly. He'd learned over the years that any sentient species had a boundless capacity for cruelty. He had once wondered if humanity alone could be so brutal, but his time away from Earth had shown him emphatically that this was not so.

If that cruelty were not matched by kindness, it would be a bleak universe, indeed.

Jeltor, thankfully, had moved on to more productive things. "We have to find her," he told Barnabas. "And determine why she did this."

"I hope to have an answer to that question soon," Barnabas told him. "It looks like she might be heading to Gerris Station. It's pretty much the only thing we can think of that's within the range of that shuttle."

Jeltor bobbed in a way that seemed to indicate a nod.

Barnabas hesitated. "There's a possibility I want to prepare you for," he said as gently as he could.

Jeltor was silent.

"We've been looking at this as political murder," Barnabas said, "but it's possible that it's personal." He thought he sensed surprise and tried to explain. "Murders sometimes seem senseless, but the murderer always has a reason. This assassin didn't move like a Jotun—if I hadn't grabbed her and felt the metal, I would never have known what she was. Either she's someone with a grudge, or someone hired her, but either way, this was planned."

"I know." Jeltor sounded determined.

"You say that," Barnabas said, struggling to find the words, "but I want to prepare you for the fact that you might find out things you didn't want to know. Things that make you think of him in a different light."

He hadn't thought of that until the moment he said it, but he knew it was true. An assassin of this caliber betrayed a longstanding grudge of some sort, and there were far too many unanswered questions in Barnabas' opinion.

For one thing, if this were a political assassination, why was it *Huword* the Senate was going after? By all reports, *he* hadn't been the one who had led the mutiny. Had he provided some support or information that even most of the other naval captains didn't know about?

And if they were making a point, why not publicize it?

Assassinations left a bad taste in Barnabas' mouth. He hated those who killed to sow fear. In this case, those who had killed did not seem to be making a point of it—and that meant they were altogether subtler.

And Barnabas did not like that.

CHAPTER NINE

Jeltor sat alone in the darkness of his rooms and fought a feeling of deep worry.

When Barnabas had first called, Jeltor had not questioned the cause of Huword's murder. The Yennai Corporation had been run by some of the most unscrupulous individuals he had ever heard of, and their infiltration of the Jotun Senate had been all but complete. Jeltor knew that there were senators who would not hesitate to order naval officers assassinated.

Frankly, he was surprised they'd gotten through the past two weeks without a rash of mysterious deaths. The Senate had been eerily silent, although their rage was palpable.

But what if Barnabas was right? What if this was something else? After all, there *hadn't* been other deaths. No one had come for Jeltor, even though he might be considered the one who started all of this.

Which meant that Huword's death was likely something different in a way no one yet understood.

The thing was, Jeltor had no idea where to start looking. Had someone murdered Barnabas, for instance, Jeltor would have looked at a list of people Barnabas had judged over the years. If someone had murdered Gar, Jeltor would look at the people Gar had wronged in his climb to the near-top of the community on Devon—or associates of Lan, whom Gar had betrayed. It wasn't difficult to follow the threads, usually. Everyone had enemies, didn't they?

When it came to Huword, however, Jeltor honestly could not think of anyone.

He thought back to their time at the naval academy. Huword had been like any other person in many respects, falling in and out of love, hanging out with friends, and cultivating a reputation for good work. He was funnier than most people Jeltor knew, but that was hardly anything Jeltor could imagine might result in his death. Not everyone liked a comedian, but those people just hung out with more serious people, didn't they?

Briefly, he considered that Huword had done this to himself, somehow. Perhaps he'd been distraught over his demotion to the *Gar'aemon*? If he thought his career was over and he'd been ruined, would he do something like that? Hire someone to disconnect his suit?

No. It made no sense. Why not leave a note? Why *any* of the little details that abounded in this case?

But that led Jeltor to an interesting theory: Huword's demotion. Perhaps it *was* something to do with that.

That thought gave him a burst of energy and he went into motion, pulling up every communication he'd ever had from Huword and poring back over the records of their academy days. He saw videos of their training and mentions of tests and debates; anyone who hoped to be an admiral was required to show top marks in military strategy. Like all of them, Huword had hoped to be an admiral.

And, like most of them, he hadn't made it. Jeltor sat still for a long time, trying to remember if Huword had seemed uncommonly upset about that.

He couldn't remember. Huword had always been very good-natured.

None of this made *sense.* Jeltor groaned aloud. He wished he could think of a single fact that made *any* of this make sense, but the more he thought, the more muddled he became. Huword had gotten along with everyone. He was clever, he was funny, he could listen to anyone kindly. After all, who had Jeltor gone to after all of his breakups or bad tests? Huword. He always had a bottle of something and a sympathetic ear.

Something occurred to Jeltor then. It was something he couldn't quite put his finger on, more like an itch in his mind than actual thought, and he found himself flipping feverishly through pictures on the screen, little video clips, messages—anything he could find.

He'd know it when he saw it, wouldn't he? He'd be able to recognize it when he saw whatever it was his mind was trying to tell him...wouldn't he?

As it happened, he did.

"You are cleared to dock." The Brakalon voice sounded strange through the translation filter, and Norwun could

hear the actual growl and hiss of the Brakalon language in the background.

Brakalons. He grimaced. They were everything he hated: big and brawny, preferring to solve their problems with muscle rather than thought.

It wasn't just a cultural distaste, though. When a Brakalon went off the rails, there was a good chance of someone getting hurt—and what chance did a Jotun have of surviving if their tank was breached?

Not a very good one, out here.

He and his team intended to complete their mission very quickly.

Norwun got up from the pilot's seat and looked at his compatriots. There were five of them on this team, all outfitted with specialized suits that would let them hook into the systems of the *Srisa*...among other things. As Norwun looked at them, one was retracting a needle into a leg panel, and another was folding a knife down onto the inside of a forearm plate.

They did not say anything. They had been briefed. They would be awaiting Norwun's orders because until he knew what had occurred after the murder, he would not know what must be done.

He would prefer to avoid the deaths of everyone aboard the *Srisa*, of course—in a general way. He felt no real emotion at the thought. Sometimes people needed to die. Sometimes he needed to be the one to kill them. He was vaguely aware that many others made a fuss about such things, but he believed it was an act.

When the doors opened, they found a hulking Brakalon waiting for them in the corridor. The *thing*—Norwun could not tell if it was male or female, and he did not care to figure it out—ducked its head in a crude greeting.

"I am Captain Kelnamon," it said. "I am glad you were able to dock safely. There has been trouble."

"Yes," Norwun said shortly. "The body is this way?"

"Yes." The captain hurried to accompany him.

"You said there was trouble," Norwun said. He did not like the sound of that. The devices blocking the distress signal had still been up when his crew arrived, but their ship had not been—and there was the trace of a self-destruct. What that meant, Norwun was not sure.

But if the Brakalon understood what had happened, if he had seen too much...

Norwun did not exchange a glance with any of the others. They were all professionals. They were paying attention.

"Yes." The Brakalon cleared his throat anxiously. "A ship was nearby, apparently blocking the distress signal and also taking down ships that tried to approach us. It destroyed a Brakalon government ship." He sounded angry now.

Despite himself, Norwun felt a flicker of worry. He was waiting for the Brakalon to lose control, he realized, and unleash a wave of violence that might cause quite a bit of damage. Norwun was well-trained and quite lethal—but there was always the chance of something going very wrong. Fights were chaotic.

"Did the ship leave?" he asked finally. It was not a good sign that the captain had said no more on the subject.

"No, it was apprehended. Well..." The Brakalon cleared his throat. "I'm given to understand that it self-destructed."

Norwun tried to parse this. "I'm sorry, what do you mean by that? Did you not see it?"

"No." The Brakalon was looking at him worriedly. He paused, considered, and said finally, "Perhaps our customs are unknown to you. When a murder has occurred, it is the responsibility of law enforcement to deal with the problem." He paused again. "I am, of course, prepared to turn the investigation over to you, although it is already in progress."

"And what are your findings?" Norwun asked silkily.

"Not *my* findings," the Brakalon told him. "It is being investigated by a human."

"A *human*?" No. Oh, no. And then, even though Norwun knew, he had to ask: "What is the human's name?"

"Barnabas," the Brakalon said. He seemed to be studying Norwun carefully. He stopped at a door in the hallway and nodded into the room. "This is where the body is."

Norwun stood in quiet horror. This was so, so much worse than he had imagined. He had guessed when the guard ship had gone silent that they might need to eliminate certain witnesses. He had anticipated venting the *Srisa*. They would take care of things quietly; the Brakalons need never know. It could have been pirates, after all.

But if Barnabas was involved...

And the *Shinigami* wasn't here, so where in the nineteen hells of Baletoth was Barnabas *now*?

"How does the investigation proceed, then?" he asked finally, trying to control his voice.

"That, I don't know." The Brakalon sounded genuinely regretful. "As I said, the government should be responsible for investigations. Since I was on the ship when it happened, I am technically a suspect, and my actions in breaking the tank certainly contaminated the scene. As soon as it became clear that this was a violent death, I locked the scene to further intervention and notified both the Jotun and Brakalon governments." He sounded worried. "I wish I had more to tell you, but I thought it best that the scene remain closed so there would be no disturbances. For the sake of clues, you understand."

Norwun fought not to snort in annoyance. Of course, he understood how investigations went. Did the Brakalon think he was so stupid?

He should not be upset, however, because it sounded as if it were possible—just possible—that no one on the ship knew what was going on. And that was very good for all of them since it might just buy them their lives.

Norwun would have been tempted to kill them all anyway, except that Barnabas was now involved. He had a reputation for oversized reactions whenever civilians died.

"And the crew?" Norwun asked. "The passengers?"

"We have communicated the delays, but not the cause." The Brakalon shrugged, looking defeated. "They are very angry, but what can I do? There are protocols."

"Why did you turn the investigation over to Barnabas?"

"Ah." The captain now looked very worried indeed. "It should have been one of our two governments, yes? I know. But it had already been a week, and the Brakalon ship had not arrived, and I had not heard from the Jotun government. I feared that if I stalled for much longer, the murderer might strike again."

"So you believe this was a random murder?" Norwun

asked neutrally. That was an interesting idea. It looked like they might not be able to stay ahead of the news at this point, but it was possible that they could spin it as a chance occurrence, a game of cards gone wrong—

Yes, it was possible. Barnabas was the loose end there, but perhaps even he could be convinced.

They had to get off this ship, and quickly. All he needed to know was whether these people had to die.

"Who can say?" the captain asked. "Perhaps it was not random, but then why would it happen here? It doesn't make any sense. No one would know he was here."

"Did he not have any traveling companions?" They'd been having the devil of a time figuring out if anyone else had been involved.

The Brakalon hesitated again. "There was another captain—Ferqar."

Norwun hoped he managed to conceal the leap of his interest.

"As he was the traveling companion, I needed to find him to move him to another cabin. When I went to where he was, the bartender told me that he had been there over the whole time period when the murder might have occurred—not that I told him why I was asking. I know I shouldn't have, of course, but...you know, when there are only two Jotuns on board, you wonder about the other one, yes? I didn't think anyone else knew him." The Brakalon's shoulders slumped. "But I knew I shouldn't investigate— and now Ferqar is gone."

"He's *gone*?"

"Perhaps Barnabas took him. He left very suddenly. I haven't received clearance from the Brakalon government to move yet, so we must stay. I wish he'd told us what was going on..."

Give thanks to all your gods that he didn't, Norwun thought acerbically. He gestured to the others to go around the captain and begin assessing the crime scene and retrieve the body.

"We will be gone soon," he said. "I hope you can understand that we must take the body."

"Oh, of course. Of course." The Brakalon nodded eagerly. "It is rightfully your investigation instead of Barnabas'. Should I set up a channel for you to speak to him and ask him to return with his information?"

No! The urge to yell was strong. Norwun took a deep breath to steady himself.

"No, thank you," he said as calmly as he could. "We will contact him. I believe we have recently been contacted by his ship, so he may be aware of our presence already. Thank you for all your help."

The Brakalon nodded. "I hope we get clearance to move soon," he said wearily. "This is playing hell with my profits. I'll go now. Let me know if you need me for anything."

"Mmm." Norwun watched him leave.

Fool. The whole species was composed of fools. It was convenient for him, of course, but still tiring to navigate.

"What should we do next?" asked Hynom, one of his associates.

"I'll tell you on the ship," Norwun said curtly.

Step one was to find Barnabas and determine what he knew. Step two was to decide if they should come back here and do some cleanup after all. For now, they could leave the *Srisa*. Best not to necessitate a diplomatic event unless there was no other option.

He knew where they'd be, anyway.

As the Jotun ship flew away, Captain Kelnamon kept his eyes fixed on the dwindling speck.

He doubted that Barnabas had everything he needed from the scene of the crime, but there wasn't anything Kelnamon could have done in this instance.

He'd known the second that ship made contact that something unusual was going on. None of the usual diplomatic protocol was on display, although there were some telltales that this was official business.

And something about those suits said that it was the sort of official business that ended with a lot of dead people, so Kelnamon had done the only thing he could think of: lied like crazy. No, he didn't know anything. No, no one knew anything. No, the other Jotun was gone. No, he couldn't move the ship until they got word from the Brakalon government. He'd even managed to change the passenger manifest while they were getting the body. There would be no useful data for them if they looked at it.

And if they ever came back, Kelnamon planned to be long gone. He gave it time for the Jotun ship to be well out of range, and then he nodded to the helmsman. The *Srisa's* engines flared, and the ship powered away into the black, going as fast as possible in the other direction.

CHAPTER TEN

"You have *got* to be kidding me," Barnabas said for what felt like the tenth time. He was hurrying along one of the lower corridors of the *Shinigami* toward the engine room. "You don't even *have* fuel lines, do you?"

"I'm telling you, I have tubes full of something, and they're less full of it than they should be. Believe me or not, I don't care, but let's at least check it out before we go kablooey."

"While the assassin gets away."

"Okay, how about this?" Shinigami projected a hologram of herself walking alongside Barnabas. She'd put on a cape today, which she'd layered over plate armor—showing, in Barnabas' opinion, that she'd never worn plate armor before in her life. No one who'd worn the stuff of necessity would ever wear it by choice.

On the other hand, as a collection of pixels, one had a great deal more leeway regarding outfits.

"How about this," she repeated. "We stop at Gerris Station, I put a few locks on all the ships, we dash back to

Border Station 7, get everything done there, and when we come back, Gerris is still in chaos, and the assassin hasn't gotten out yet."

Barnabas sighed. "I don't like it."

"Do you like *anything?*"

"I like juice."

"You sound like a toddler."

"Fine. I like quiet nights with a book, a good mug of beer, and a garden full of freshly-tilled earth."

Shinigami stopped in her tracks and blinked at him.

"What?" he asked.

"I always forget you were a monk."

After a moment of consideration, Barnabas lifted his shoulders with a wistful smile. "Sometimes I do, too. That's all very far away these days. I don't miss everything about that time, but...sometimes I miss the afternoons. The light would slant into the gardens in just the right way." He started walking again, more slowly. "It was beautiful in every season. In the spring, there was the promise of greenery. You could smell it in the air even with snow on the ground. In summer, everything was growing and flowering. The air was full of good smells from the herbs we grew. In the autumn, it was harvest—bounty and...grief, almost, the sense of winter approaching and the plants dying even as they gave fruit. And in the winter, everything was quiet. We all need quiet. Contemplation."

Shinigami said nothing for a long moment. Barnabas looked at her, still half in his memories, and she quirked her mouth to the side.

"You're a dork." She said it affectionately, he noticed.

"Mmm. Maybe I'll put in a garden."

"Where are you going to have a garden? High Tortuga?"

"On the ship. We have more than enough space. I'll fill one of the rooms with dirt." It wasn't a very workable idea, but her look of horror was worth it. *She* didn't know he wasn't serious, after all. "And I'll go along with the lock plan."

"That's good," Shinigami said serenely, "because I already did it."

Barnabas sighed.

Federation Border Station 7 was, Barnabas had to admit, a welcome taste of home. On alien space stations, he had to keep himself on guard constantly. One could never tell what might give offense, or who might want to make a point by killing a human.

The *Shinigami's* maintenance problem was clucked over by Helen Harari, one of Bobcat's former trainee mechanics who had devised a few of the *Shinigami's* systems before the Federation days, and who now went wherever she was needed to repair the far-flung ships.

"Yeah, this isn't too much of a surprise," she reported. Her voice was muffled, emerging from a compartment that she'd wedged herself inside with a flashlight and a series of antiquated looking tools.

"It's a state-of-the-art ship," Barnabas said. "How can it have problems like this? Doesn't it...self-repair?"

Helen stuck her head out to give him a look. "Some of the time, yes. Shinigami maintains the computer systems, and can even make minor repairs to hardware. But materials break down. *Especially* when you've been using a ship as hard as *you* seem to be using this one. Hell, I'd have you bring it in for maintenance every month if I thought you'd listen."

She disappeared back into the compartment with Barnabas staring after her, chagrinned.

"Anyway, go on," she called, her voice still muffled. "This won't take too long—although I'd like to get a full diagnostic in if you can spare the time."

"Sorry, not today." Barnabas fought the urge to pace in circles. "We need to be getting back to Gerris before our target finds a way through Shinigami's ship locks."

"There's always something," Helen muttered. "The next time I ask, I'm sure it will be something else urgent. Well, go on, and I'll do what I can."

Somewhat self-consciously, Barnabas set off for the main concourse. He didn't have anything, in particular, he wanted to see, but he could take the chance to have a relaxing stroll, couldn't he?

Barnabas—Jeltor says he has a message for you.

Oh?

He says he needs to tell you in person.

Barnabas stopped dead and was run into by several people. Apologizing—he was used to the near-empty hallways of the *Shinigami*—he drew into an alcove and considered. They couldn't leave just yet. Even if Barnabas weren't worried about the *Shinigami* breaking down, he wouldn't want to get a tongue-lashing from Helen.

Still, his worries about being stuck here had just doubled.

Could he meet us at Gerris Station? he asked Shinigami.

I'll pass that along.

Is it serious, do you think? Barnabas started walking again, trying to get rid of his nervous energy by moving. *Stupid question. I know it's serious. But if it's so serious, why does he think we'll be able to meet in person?*

No idea. I suppose there's a chance he's misinterpreting something or thinks it's more serious than it is, though. You organic life forms do that a lot.

Thank you for the vote of confidence.

It was meant to be reassuring.

Mmm. Barnabas was smiling, however, as he emerged into the relatively open markets. He inhaled the familiar smells of human food and felt a little bit more at home than he had in weeks.

Are you doing anything right now?

No, why?

Grainger wondered if you'd speak to the Magistrates.

Are they here? Barnabas was surprised. The Magistrates had been training to be Rangers—except, with the dissolution of the Empire, they had not finished. Barnabas remembered following their progress somewhat distractedly, but he had been off on his missions and had not kept close tabs. *Is this where they... Ah, right, it is. I could talk to them. Wait, why?*

He thought it would be good for them to see you. He says he knows you're still basically a Ranger, soooo...

You've definitely been talking with Tabitha too much. All right, where am I going?

Level 8, Room 1430. Hold on. She flashed a map for a few seconds, confusingly embedded in his vision. *Did that work?*

Yes. Yes, it did. Also, never do that again, I have a gigantic headache.

We'll fine-tune it.

That would require us to do it again.

It will be a useful thing to have down, and you know it. And I'll tell Grainger you'll be there in a couple of minutes. With that, Shinigami appeared to have vanished from his head.

"Stubborn AIs," Barnabas muttered as he headed for Level 8.

It took him a bit longer than Shinigami had advised, and he popped into the room to find several people staring expectantly at the door.

He remembered Buster at once as the man came over to shake his hand, elbowing Grainger aside. Tall and broad-shouldered, he had blond hair and blue eyes, and a thin white scar at the top of his head. Before the Rangers had disbanded, it had been the plan for Buster to do his first Ranger missions with Barnabas. But all of that had gone out the window when Barnabas headed off on his own. Barnabas had felt a bit guilty about that, but Buster seemed to have landed on his feet just fine.

Also, it would not have made sense for him to bring someone else on this mission. At the time, he had needed to work on his own and chart his own course.

The others were less familiar, but he vaguely remembered some faces.

"Please, take a seat and share some words of wisdom," Grainger offered. As tall as Buster, he had silvery scars that remained from his time as a Ranger. Even a werewolf couldn't heal from some of the types of trouble Rangers found. His blue eyes were warm, and his face held the calm competence Barnabas most missed from his time in the Empire.

He shook everyone's hands, half his thoughts still absorbed with the investigation. He needed to get back to Gerris Station and see what Jeltor had come across.

A woman with bright, inquisitive eyes shook Barnabas' hand, and something flashed in her gaze—curiosity, and understanding. Barnabas remembered talk of one of the trainees who could read thoughts on physical contact. Rivka, was it? He'd ask later.

He took a seat at last and tried to think of something to say. He smiled at the group. "Words of wisdom. Hmm." He looked up at the ceiling and considered. "Well, you'll have an idea about the missions, but no one tells you the shit you'll be putting up with from everyone else—bureaucrats, low-level station administrators, bankers. And the past few missions, I've had a crew of gloriously incompetent pirates trying to steal my ship."

"Talk to us about your current mission. I sense it's bothering you. Maybe we can help. We have some resources," Rivka politely suggested.

Grainger looked at her, his brow furrowing slightly. He seemed curious but not worried.

"Ah. I suppose I could do that." Barnabas gave her an intrigued look before settling back in his seat. Yes, she probably *had* seen something in his thoughts. In any case, it could hardly hurt to see what they might say, and even if they had no suggestions, they'd be well-served by seeing that there were missions with no easy places to start. "We responded to a distress call from a civilian ship. Now, this was far out—well out of Federation territory. They know of humans there, but not well, and there are a few species you might not know: Brakalons, Ubuara, Luvendi, Jotun."

The group all leaned forward to listen, eager to hear more.

"A Jotun was murdered on the transport," Barnabas explained. "Now, the Jotun are—well, they sort of look like jellyfish, so what they do is they make these mechanical suits that have a tank in the middle of them. They kind of float there and control the suit with their tentacles."

"That's crazy," Buster breathed.

"No, what's *crazy* is trying to tell them apart." Barnabas flashed him a smile.

You are not kidding, Shinigami commented. *I've been working on a mapping algorithm to tell the most minute differences and still nothing.*

I've started looking at the suits—scratches, that sort of thing.

Clever human.

There's an art to making a patronizing comment, you know —and I have to say, you have it down.

"Anyway, the ship had to be brought to a halt because under Brakalon law, if a crime happens on a spaceship, you have to stop the whole thing and wait for authorities to arrive. Well…there was a complication."

"Isn't there always?" Grainger muttered.

Barnabas gave a low laugh. "Every single time, I swear. So, the first thing that happened was we showed up, and there was a spaceship a little ways away from the *Srisa*, trying to block the distress signal and shooting down any ship that tried to approach."

The group looked at each other, intrigued by this development.

"It was an advanced craft, and probably would have taken down any other ship easily, but—well, the *Shinigami* was Bethany Anne's personal ship." Barnabas gave a small, self-satisfied smile. "It was easy to evade what this ship was throwing at us and tail them. We figured we'd be able to unravel the murder easily, except that the alien flying it used a self-destruct protocol rather than talk to us."

"Over a single murder?" Rivka demanded. "Who was this person?"

"Interesting question. I assume you mean the murdered Jotun, yes?" Barnabas waited for her nod. "Yes, he was a ship captain in the Jotun Navy. Now, something you probably won't know—I worked with the Jotun Navy on my last mission, and that was against the direct orders of their Senate. Long story short, we were going up against a corporation that had bribed some of the senators to look the other way, and the Navy wasn't willing to. One of our best theories is that the murdered captain helped in the battle, and the Senate had him killed. But there are some issues with that theory."

"They'd have publicized it if they did, wouldn't they?" Rivka pointed out. "Because they'd want it to be a warning, right? Or a very public punishment, at least."

"That's a good point." Barnabas frowned. "Also strange is the fact that the other ship waited by the *Srisa*. They didn't take the actual assassin and leave, and the assassin didn't shut down the *Srisa*'s distress signal. It's as if the two weren't working together—but both of them wanted what they were doing to be kept quiet."

The group looked at one another.

"Well, he *was* involved in something shady," Buster said

finally. He shrugged and looked around at the others. "Right? He had to be. He screwed someone over hard, probably with someone else. The assassin killed him quietly—"

"Why, though?" Rivka interrupted.

"I don't know, but let me finish. So they killed him quietly, and the other ship was there because his accomplices suspected that was why he was killed, and they didn't want anyone to find out about it. They were going to try to hush it up, you know?"

Barnabas was staring at him, frowning slightly. An idea was clearly coming to him. "They sent a message to the Jotun government," he said slowly. "The captain of the *Srisa* said he had sent a message. I assumed it was to the Navy— but what if he sent it to the Senate?"

Buster gave him a deer-in-the-headlights look. "I'm not sure I quite—"

"We all thought he was assassinated by the Senate for helping the Navy," Barnabas explained. "But what if he was assassinated by the Navy for helping the Senate?" He slapped his leg. "That's it. That's absolutely it. They sent that ship to keep anyone from investigating until their own people could get to it. Oh, Jeltor is not going to be happy." He rubbed his face and stood. "I...have to go right now, I'm afraid. There are some people I need to talk to before any more assassins get hired. Thank you all." He ran for the doorway and pelted through it, only to stick his head back around the doorframe a moment later. "It was very nice to meet all of you. I hope we'll meet again, and if you're ever in need of aid, do call on the *Shinigami*."

He left, sprinting for his ship.

Shinigami! I've got it! Did you hear that?

Hmm? Sorry, I was keeping tabs on the ships at Gerris. They're freaking out. What's going on?

Huword! He wasn't helping the Navy, he was helping the Senate.

Whoa, wait. Shinigami sounded skeptical. *Is there evidence of that?*

We'll find evidence. Tell you what, I will bet you three pairs of those shoes with the red on the bottom—

Louboutins. Jesus, it is not *that hard to remember.*

Focus. Barnabas swung himself around the door of the docking bay. *Three pairs of those. That's what Jeltor is going to tell us on Gerris. Wait, did he say he's coming?*

Yep. He'll meet us there. Also, may I point out that there are *no more Louboutins in the world? I want Tasper Dells. They're the best ones now.*

Fine. I can do that. Do we have a bet?

We have a bet.

CHAPTER ELEVEN

They knew where she was. Somehow, they already knew. In the tiny, dingy room she'd rented, Kantar paced back and forth.

She didn't want to admit it, but she was terrified. Even the act of moving in her biosuit, pacing, knowing she appeared as graceful and natural as any other life form, did not help her anxiety.

That was because it didn't *help* her now. Nothing would help until she could get herself off this station, and she had no idea how to do that.

She had thought the station administrator was stalling —that they'd taken a bribe and would be coming for her. If someone had wanted to find her, after all, that would have been the easiest way. She'd docked with a shuttle, which was noteworthy, and keeping any ships from going on or off the station would have been a nice, simple way to keep her in place while they hunted her down.

And then...none of that had happened. The Jotuns had never had a violent dictatorship, thank all the gods, but

Kantar had traveled enough that she knew how these things went: banging on the doors at night, people stopped at checkpoints, posted rewards for information on anyone suspicious.

She'd stayed awake the first night with a gun trained on the door. Unlike a more standard life form, she could set the suit in one position and have it wake her up as soon as there was a disturbance outside.

She'd been too nervous to sleep, though. She'd been *sure* they were coming for her.

No one came. No one came the next day, either, and when she finally steeled herself to speak to the station administrator, she found a line that went out of the offices and wound around the markets. Ship captains were irate, minor dignitaries on the ships were irate, traders in perishable goods were especially irate, and no one seemed to be leaving the offices any happier than they'd been upon entering.

When Kantar finally made her way through the line, she found out why. She was met by a secretary who had set up camp in the hallway in a hastily-constructed booth. In fact, every member of the station administrator's staff, down to someone who looked like part of the cleaning crew, was presently explaining to people in the line that there was nothing they could do and no bribe that would be sufficient to release a ship.

By the end of the conversation, Kantar even believed that they were telling her the truth. At this point, with so many people irate and willing to spend astronomical bribes, surely *someone* would have cracked.

But that meant that someone had overridden the entire

station system and locked all the ships in place—and that hardly made Kantar feel better. The Senate was coming for her—she knew it.

She wasn't stupid, of course. She had always known this was a possibility. She wasn't, strictly speaking, an assassin —not until now, anyway. She was just someone who was able to get into unusual places and do unusual things because she wasn't what she appeared to be. A friend of a friend who knew her had passed along the job, and she'd taken it for free because she knew it was the right thing to do—to kill Huword.

Some people needed to die for the things they'd done. She believed that.

Yes, she had known it might kill her. The thing was, she wasn't quite ready to die.

So how in hell did she get off this station before they found her?

———

"Where does that leave us?" The voice on the other end of the comm was unimpressed.

Norwun tried not to lose himself to disquiet. In general, he preferred it when people got angry and yelled a lot. When they were displeased but very quiet, situations tended to be more dangerous. Those people held grudges.

Those people killed you later, very deliberately and very painfully.

So far, Norwun had managed to avoid that fate, and he was hoping to keep the streak going. So he was careful to modulate his voice when he replied.

"It's a very good situation. Well, as good as it can be."

"And how," the other voice said, "did you reach that conclusion?" They were speaking even more calmly now, which set the alarm bells off in Norwun's head.

Norwun pretended that he couldn't think of any reason things would be wrong. "Whoever killed Huword hasn't made very much of it, have they? It's still quiet, and we can spin it however we need to. There aren't any loose ends on the *Srisa*, which means we don't need to worry about a Brakalon civilian ship going missing. That could have been messy. And of all the aliens to pick up the trail, it's one who was already an enemy. There's no need to worry that someone else has any information."

There was silence, and Norwun found himself praying silently. *Please agree, please agree.*

"I suppose you're right." There was genuine surprise in the voice.

Norwun bobbed slightly in relief, tentacles going slack for a moment. He hadn't yet determined just who he was speaking to within the Senate, which made him nervous. They had the correct clearance to be able to contact him, which meant they must be the head of one of the committees, but they hadn't told him which one and he had the feeling that if he asked, they would not be pleased.

"On the other hand," the senator said, sending Norwun back into a quiet frenzy of anxiety, "Barnabas is already determined to find damaging information on the Senate."

"He already *has* damaging information," Norwun countered. The confrontation in the Senate had not been widely publicized, but Norwun had, of course, heard of it. Barnabas had made threats that made it clear he knew exactly what had happened between the Senate and the Yennai Corporation. "He hasn't made it public."

"Do *not* make the mistake of thinking he's harmless." The senator's voice was harsh. "The Yennai Corporation made that mistake, and they are gone. Their *fleet* is gone. They were one of the most powerful entities in this sector, and there is nothing left of them. He disassembled them piece by piece. If we allow him to continue on this path, there is no telling what he might find...or disrupt."

There was something there. Norwun pondered it. He had learned to read between the lines of what senators said, for the simple reason that they usually didn't come out and tell him what to do—he had to puzzle out their meaning.

It confused him, back in the day. He had almost made several costly mistakes by not realizing that they wanted people killed or interrogated. Luck had gotten him through those times, and he had learned how to interpret their words.

In this case, the senator had admitted something without meaning to. They were worried Barnabas would find something specific and disrupt things, and it had nothing to do with the bribes the Yennai Corporation had been giving them. So what was it?

This was very interesting, and Norwun wanted to know what it was about—if only from the perspective of self-preservation.

Unfortunately, it was difficult enough to find shadowy secrets when you knew whose secrets you were investigating. Without knowing so much as the name of his contact, his chances of discovering their secrets were essentially nil.

Sometimes he wished he'd chosen a different job—a shop clerk, maybe. An engineer. Something where your employer didn't kill you if things went wrong.

Maybe he'd look into that.

For now, he said simply, "Barnabas has a weakness. He will not let civilians be killed. This can be used to trap him."

"Others have tried that." The senator sounded unimpressed.

"As you say, others underestimate him. I won't. His ship is part of his invincibility. I will separate him from it. I will constrain him somewhere that he cannot use violent force for fear of harming civilians around him. Then I will kill him without fighting him directly. That was the problem others had; they tried to fight, and he can fight any number of opponents successfully. Put him somewhere there's nothing to fight—where his opponent is the lack of air or heat—and we'll have more luck."

It was more than he'd wanted to reveal. He usually tried to be vague so that if there were any changes to the plan on the fly, he could claim he'd meant to do those things all along.

In this case, however, the specifics seemed to reassure his contact.

"Good," he said simply. "Deal with him quickly, then follow up with the *Srisa*. I want it destroyed."

"But..." Norwun began to be even more worried. "No one on the ship knew anything."

"So they said. Perhaps it is even true after a fashion. But there's no knowing what they might have seen and what might become relevant later. I said I wanted it destroyed, and I want every passenger dealt with."

There was only one answer. "Yes, of course."

The call ended, and Norwun stared around the bridge, trying to calm himself. He'd killed like this before without remorse, but always for a *purpose*. This was now turning into a plan for wholesale slaughter, and he didn't like it. As much as it bothered him to think he might have an emotional weakness, it seemed he did.

He wished there was anything to be done about it.

He didn't think there was, though. He knew his place. He carried out orders or was killed himself. The senator would survive either way and find someone else to do what Norwun wouldn't.

Those people were as good as dead. He might as well be the one to do it.

Jeltor checked the navigational computer for the seventh time, the backup navigational computer for the twelfth time, and the scopes for the fifty-eighth time before relaxing enough to get out of his chair and open the door to the back portion of the spacecraft.

He still wasn't exactly relaxed, but on the other hand—

"What the hell is this about?" his wife demanded.

Jeltor, who had thought his family would still be under the effects of the tranquilizers he'd slipped them, jumped.

"What is what about?" he asked as nonchalantly as he could.

"We're all on a spaceship," his wife said, "and if you thought I wouldn't notice that, you should never have been allowed to pilot a ship in the Navy because you're unforgivably stupid. As it is, I can see you preparing to lie your way out of this, so I'll give you some advice. Don't even try."

"Right. Erm, out of curiosity, how *are* you awake?" There was a beep behind him, and Jeltor spun around in his tank to look—but it was only an automated message to tell him that they were approaching an asteroid belt, exactly in the time frame they should be.

His wife snorted. "I got my suit upgraded. It deals with any chemicals I haven't told it I'm going to be taking."

"That's a nice upgrade." He wished she'd mentioned that. He was about to get the mother of all lectures, and he didn't want to explain what was going on.

To his surprise, she didn't yell. "Jeltor, in all our years together, you've never done anything like this. I can't imagine you did this to hurt us. You must have thought we were in danger. What's going on?"

Jeltor gave his children a worried look. They *were* still out cold. "Let's talk in the cockpit."

They closed the door behind them. Jeltor wondered where exactly he should begin.

"You remember when Barnabas called me?" he said finally.

"Yes."

"Captain Huword—you remember him?—was murdered. On a Brakalon civilian transport in the middle of nowhere."

"Jeltor." She sounded sad. "I'm so sorry. I know you two were close."

He fought a wave of bitterness. "We really weren't," he explained. "I thought we were, but we weren't. It was good that I hadn't seen him since everything started with the Yennai Corporation, because I might have been murdered instead."

She fell silent, radiating surprise.

Jeltor swallowed and tried to find the words.

In the end, though, it was easier than he expected: "Huword was a traitor," he said bluntly, "and I would have killed him myself if I'd had the chance."

CHAPTER TWELVE

Showered, changed, his stomach full of delicious food, and with a break in his case, Barnabas was in a much better mood when he went onto the bridge of the *Shinigami* a few hours later.

Unfortunately, he found himself in the middle of a heated argument between Shinigami and the administrator of Gerris station. Gar was sitting wide-eyed, apparently not trusting the outcome if he were to speak up, while Shinigami had taken to hissing human expletives in various non-English languages.

Tafa, who was seated in the pilot's chair, swiveled around to give Barnabas a surprisingly cheerful nod. After a moment, Barnabas decided that meant everything was under control. Tafa had grown up as part of a family that executed anyone they didn't like, so if she was fine with the situation, it was a good sign that the raised voices were just that—loud, nothing worse.

Barnabas decided to enjoy the show.

"Listen, *afatottari*," Shinigami said sweetly, "*cagati in mano e prenditi a schiaffi, si?* I don't *care* if ships can't undock. That's not what I'm trying to do."

Gar leaned over. "What is she saying?"

"Well, I didn't understand the first bit," Barnabas admitted, "but I did understand the Italian and let's just say it wasn't very, err…hygienic, as suggestions go."

"You are not understanding," the station administrator said. He sounded quite harried at this point. "If you dock with us, I cannot verify that you will be able to undock. Several ships have tried and been severely damaged—and they have not managed to get clear of the station."

Shinigami gave Barnabas a look. *Stupid motherfucker.*

Just lock down the station, you said. Barnabas was enjoying this. *Simple, you said. I've already done it, you said.*

Oh, sure, and I'm *the one who hangs out too much with Tabitha. I think I liked it better when you had a stick up your ass.*

I beg your pardon?

Hey, there it is again. She looked back at the screen. "How about this? We're going to dock with your station. You can either allow us to do so at a docking port or we will find a place that looks promising and drill through the side of the station. And if you don't like either of those two options, *chupe mantequilla de mi culo.*"

"We *cannot* allow you to dock!"

"*Hijo de las mil putas.*" Shinigami dropped her head into one hand.

"Hello," Barnabas said pleasantly. "This is the captain of the *Shinigami.* May I presume I'm speaking to Westo Gor'rathi?"

"Yes." By this point, the man seemed to have lost hope

of leaving the conversation unscathed. Had he understood Shinigami, Barnabas suspected he'd have come to that conclusion much earlier.

Barnabas settled back in his chair. "I have on board an exceedingly talented network specialist who may be able to untangle whatever problem is presently occurring in your systems. In the meantime, I give you my word that neither I nor my affiliates will hold you responsible for any issues we may have relating to your present problems."

The station administrator said nothing in response.

"What do you have to lose?" Barnabas asked reasonably. "So there will be one more crew on your station. A drop in the bucket. And there's the chance we can fix your problem."

There was a long pause.

"*Fine,*" the station manager said savagely. "Dock at Bay 78. And tell your first mate to *hoje nad'razg hujkira.*"

The line cut and Barnabas looked at Shinigami, who shrugged.

"If he wants to shock me, he's going to have to try harder than that. Definitely passing that one on to Tabitha, though."

"What did it mean? Actually, no, do *not* tell me—"

"Well, they have more orifices than we do—"

"I SAID, DON'T TELL ME."

Had she remained holed up in her room, Kantar might not have heard about the two new ships. As it was, she heard people on the station threatening to start a riot and decided to investigate.

"It's ridiculous!" a Torcellan female hissed at her companion. "We'll run out of food soon, and they're letting new ships dock?"

Kantar froze, her mind racing ahead.

"It could be supply ships," the other one said reasonably.

"It was a frigate and a personal ship," the first one shot back. "And one of them was *Jotun*, of all things—or at least, that's what Yednamor said."

Oh, no.

The second Torcellan didn't look convinced, but Kantar was. She pushed her way through the crowd and tried not to break into a sprint. She couldn't afford to be noteworthy, not now.

But if they were here, it was only a matter of time until they came for her, wasn't it?

She knew what she had to do.

They emerged into chaos. Gar, still habitually inclined to stay away from unpredictable crowds, froze in the doorway of the ship and wouldn't move until Tafa took his hand and led him into the landing bay, murmuring soothingly.

"Awww," Shinigami said quietly to Barnabas.

He nodded in agreement. He still wasn't quite sure what had prompted him to offer Tafa a spot on his ship, and he suspected that most of it was nothing more than sentiment. When he'd found her, she'd been a hostage with

Jeltor. She'd stopped believing that the universe was a place where good things happened. She had no skill in combat, nor did she have any desire to learn.

In short, she was hardly a logical addition to a Ranger's crew. She'd been useful, however, showing a talent for a surprising range of things from data manipulation to piloting. When Barnabas had returned to Helen's workshop on Station 7 he'd found Tafa wedged into the compartment with the human mechanic, learning about the *Shinigami's* internal workings and fixing a hose under Helen's watchful eye.

And there were things like this, too—Tafa talking things over with her shipmates and, in general, making the ship a nicer place to be.

Barnabas hoped she stayed around. Truly good people, in his opinion, were few and far between. When you found one, you hung onto them as long as you could.

"Barnabas!" Jeltor came clanking around the edge of the doorway. "I just saw Tafa and Gar. They said they're going to find some juice. Do they mean batteries?"

"No, they mean that Barnabas has an unfortunate addiction." Shinigami tried to roll her eyes but didn't quite have the trick of it yet. It looked truly frightening.

"Where do you want to speak?" Barnabas asked when Jeltor looked confused.

"Ah. On your ship, if possible." Jeltor looked around. "Anyone here could be listening in." He hesitated. "And may I bring my family aboard? I have them in crates so no one will see them on the security feeds. I brought them with me since I was scared of what might happen if I left them."

"Of course." Barnabas nodded at Shinigami, who went off to make the arrangements. His heart gave a pang. "I'm sorry you've been so worried. I promise we won't let anyone hurt your family. And if you doubt me," he added, trying to make Jeltor smile, "remember that we took down a whole fleet together."

"Right." Jeltor didn't sound convinced, but he allowed himself to be led onto the *Shinigami*, and it was only a few minutes before they heard the clanking sounds that indicated that his family was aboard.

Shinigami joined them as a hologram a moment later. "I set them up in one of the guest suites," she explained.

"Thank you, Shinigami." Barnabas sat in one of the chairs of the main lounge area and nodded at Jeltor to speak. "You said you found something important."

"I did." Jeltor's biosuit twitched several times as though he were giving it tiny involuntary commands. Certainly, his actual body was twitching rapidly in the central tank.

That's creepy, Shinigami commented.

You know, I'd say you're being rude, but…I have to agree. Barnabas tried not to grimace.

Unaware of their discussion, Jeltor was struggling to find words. "I was wrong about everything I told you about Huword. I told you he didn't have any enemies and that he was good-natured and trustworthy, and none of that was true."

Barnabas tilted his head to the side, waiting.

"I can't prove this," Jeltor continued. "He covered his tracks well. But trust me when I say I *know* it's true. Even if I can't prove it, it all makes sense—he was working with the Senate. He's been collecting information on all of us for years, and he was just waiting for an opportunity to get ahead by using it. I can't even imagine what else he's done with it, but I know he betrayed some of the admirals. They're in front of the Senate for charges that don't sound very bad, but their careers will be gone, and they'll be ruined. And Huword was the one passing them information about the Navy's technology...which they gave to Yennai, of course."

Barnabas blew out a breath. "You know, I wondered if that might be it." *Too bad I didn't make you put something on that bet.*

Are you kidding? He doesn't have any proof. You still owe me shoes.

I said this was what he was here to tell us, and it was. No shoes.

Ugh.

"You didn't tell me?" Jeltor sounded frustrated. "You knew, and you didn't tell me?"

"I didn't suspect until after you were already on your way here, and I didn't want to say anything in case I was wrong. But with both of us arriving at this conclusion independently, I'd say it's likely we're onto something. It certainly helps the various pieces of this debacle make a bit more sense."

"Such as?" Jeltor looked confused.

"Well, there was the Jotun ship that was shooting down anyone who approached, but they didn't seem to be working with the assassin. They probably *weren't*. They were sent by the Senate, and they were trying to keep people away from the *Srisa* until the Senate's cleanup crew could arrive. Speaking of which," Barnabas frowned "I sent a message to the *Srisa* while we were on our way here but haven't heard back."

He, Shinigami, and Jeltor looked at one another, worried.

"I should never have left them there," Barnabas said quietly.

"You couldn't have known," Shinigami told him soothingly.

"As soon as I suspected this was between the Navy and the Senate, I should have assumed someone would treat that ship as a whole set of loose ends."

"No, and here's why." Shinigami locked eyes with him. "They had a ship there blocking access, but it hadn't shot the *Srisa* down. They had chances to destroy it, and they didn't. And the fact is, maybe the *Srisa* got cleared to make port somewhere. There's no way to know."

"Right." Barnabas nodded. "Yes. Right." His thoughts were still racing, but he could hope she was correct.

"So what do we do?" Jeltor asked them. He shook his head. "I don't understand any of this. No one spoke to me of it, so whoever found out what he was up to didn't set out to make an example of him. I spoke to some of the other captains who were part of the mutiny, and they're all as shocked as I was. *None* of them so much as suggested that he deserved it, and trust me, if they knew what he'd done, someone would have told me."

"That's interesting," Barnabas commented. "No one's making a big deal of this. I feel like it should be all over the news, and both the Senate and the Navy should be making statements."

"They are, but there isn't any sort of...positioning." Jeltor shook his head.

"Well, whoever he was and whatever he was up to, he was in deep." Barnabas shook his head. "And I'm guessing that the closer we look, the worse stuff we're going to find."

"I don't even want to think about it." Jeltor sounded worried.

"I hate to interrupt," Shinigami said, "but we have a situation."

"What?" Barnabas was on his feet in a moment.

"That assassin on the *Srisa*? She's here, and she's trying to get onto the ship."

Barnabas took off for the doorway.

"Don't you want armor?" Shinigami's voice projected from several speakers at once.

"I'm not going to fight her," Barnabas called back. "She's the one who understands all of what's going on!"

"Yeah, are you sure she knows you're on her side? Because she's armed to the teeth."

"I'll be able to explain," Barnabas said, annoyed. "Open the doors."

Shinigami had been right to worry, however, because as soon as the doors slid open and the assassin saw him running toward her, she only hesitated for a moment. She whipped a rifle down from over her head, aimed, and fired.

CHAPTER THIRTEEN

"Whoa!"

The assassin's biosuit was fast, but Barnabas' reactions were honed to a higher standard than the average organic life form. He threw himself sideways with a yell and collided with the wall while the bullet zoomed past him to embed itself in the back wall of the hallway behind him.

Hey! Shinigami yelled. *Get off my spaceship with that shit!* She flickered into being with a murderous expression on her face and Baba Yaga's blood-red eyes. One hand, tipped with claws, came up into the air. "You want to play?" she asked the assassin. "Let's play."

The assassin, seeing what appeared to be a vicious subspecies of human where there hadn't been one before and Barnabas *sans* bullet holes, took off like a shot.

"Not helpful, Shinigami!" Barnabas raced after her with a sigh.

Eh, you'll catch her.

As touching as your confidence is, it would be more touching if it didn't require heroics on my part. We now have a scared and highly capable assassin on a station full of civilians.

Mmm. I'm sure you'll think of something.

Barnabas shook his head and put everything he had into running. Since he had turned, he'd been stronger and faster than the average human, and Bethany Anne's well-tailored upgrades had made his body even better. He was, in essence, his perfect self, as well as having numerous other capabilities that did not, as John sometimes put it, come with the standard human package.

However, Barnabas *was* still human, and he had all the tiny imperfections that came along with that. Small variances between his left and right leg might cause tiny hitches in his stride, slowing him down. Pain might hamper him.

The Jotun assassin had none of that, and her speed was impressive. Pretty much the only saving grace for Barnabas was that she couldn't get up to any dangerous speeds when she kept having to dodge people and take corners.

At least she *was* dodging people, not pushing them out of the way or trying to take them hostage. That was a heartening sign.

"Stop!" Barnabas called. "We're on the same side!"

See, that's good. I knew you'd think of something.

It hasn't worked yet, Barnabas pointed out, *and I told the station administrator that we wouldn't cause any trouble.*

I think you knew that was bullshit when you said it.

I admit nothing. Barnabas hurdled a small stand of vegetables and detoured down a side hallway after the assassin. "Please, stop! I know why you did it!"

The assassin looked over her shoulder at that, but

whatever she saw did not reassure her. She kept running, making for the balcony that overlooked the main markets, and before Barnabas could stop her, she leaped lightly onto the railing and jumped up to grab of the next floor's railing. She hauled herself up and was gone.

Oh, hell no, Barnabas muttered internally. *You are not getting away that easily. Shinigami—*

Yeah, yeah, I'm tracking her. She's waiting to see if you climb up, I have her on the station's security cameras.

All right. Barnabas climbed up to stand on the railing and braced himself using the ceiling. "My name is Barnabas," he called. "I expect you know that. I mean you no harm."

She's getting her gun out again.

Delightful. Barnabas raised his voice. "I am following you at the behest of Captain Jeltor, who is presently on my ship."

That got her attention. She's getting closer to listen. She really does have the trick of moving like a biological life form.

"We originally believed Captain Huword's assassination to be the work of the Senate," Barnabas said, "but I think now, perhaps, that it was someone in the Navy who had him killed. And I think I know why. Huword wasn't who he appeared to be, was he? He was everyone's friend, Jeltor said. I should have known that wasn't possible. He wasn't *anyone's* friend. He was the person who listened to all their secrets and then sold them out."

It happened in the blink of an eye. The assassin swung down, landing lightly and turning to aim at Barnabas, who only just managed not to fall off the ledge.

"Don't try to get down," she said. Her voice had been

modulated to sound human now. "And tell me why I should believe you're not a Senate spy."

Barnabas started laughing. "If you'd seen my last few interactions with the Senate you wouldn't be asking that."

She did not laugh. "I *have* seen them—or heard about them, at least. I did a lot of research on you while I came here. You trapped me at this station. You locked the ships down. Why?"

"To keep you here," Barnabas admitted. "I'm sorry for the delay, but we needed maintenance on our ship. While we were doing that, I realized maybe you weren't working for the Senate. Of course, you have me at gunpoint still, so maybe I was wrong."

He'd managed to strike the right note; she was deeply offended by that.

"I am *not* working for the Senate."

Barnabas sighed. "Look, I appreciate that you're trying to stay safe, but we should *not* talk about this here. Why don't you come with me and hear me out? If you aren't willing to do so on my ship, we'll go wherever you choose. I'll bring Jeltor if you want. Or, I suppose you could speak just with him—although I warn you, if you do to him what you did to Huword, I'll hunt you down and do the same to you. Are we clear?"

She lowered the gun at last. "What's Jeltor to you?"

"A friend." Barnabas stared her down. "He was at my back when I needed help to take down the Yennai Corporation, which is something it seems like you should know, given who it was you assassinated."

She stared at him for a long moment. "You're right, we shouldn't talk here. I'll come back to your ship. Fair warning, though—if you try to get me out of this suit so you can deconstruct it or interrogate me, it will blow the whole damned station to dust."

"Mmm." *Shinigami, fact check?*

No idea, but you can bet I'll be scanning the hell out of her when she comes aboard.

We probably want to do it before.

Hmm? Oh, I didn't mean from a defensive standpoint. I want to learn how to make my *body do that.*

I should have known.

Barnabas led the way back through the station as quickly as he could. He didn't think many people had heard their conversation, and there hadn't been any violence in the station, but he still didn't want to take the chance of someone overhearing them.

In the doorway of the *Shinigami*, the assassin hesitated, and it was this, oddly, that made Barnabas relax at last. She was genuinely worried he might be trying to trap her.

"Do you know what I am?" he asked her.

"A human."

"No—well, yes—but I'm a Ranger. I seek out injustice, and I judge those who have perpetrated it. I defend the helpless." He looked at her seriously. "I could not back anyone who allied themselves either with the Yennai Corporation, or corrupt politicians."

She gave him a curious look, tilting her black-masked face to the side. Apparently, humans weren't the only species that did that. Then she seemed to remember her caution. "Show me Jeltor."

"I'm here." Jeltor clanked around the corner. "I came on a cloaked ship, watching the scopes the whole way. I was sure the Senate had somehow found out what I knew… Well, what I suspect. I have no evidence." He looked at her. "You do, though."

She stepped into the ship and let the door slide closed behind her. "And what do you suspect?"

Jeltor had to force himself to speak. He did not yet trust her. "Huword betrayed the admirals to the Senate," he said. "There's no way to know how much else he's told them. The charges are specific, and all of it is…" He shook his head. "I just want to know who found out. I don't understand why all of us weren't told."

The assassin looked at them for a long moment.

"I'm only the messenger," she said finally. "The story isn't mine to tell—and truly, I shouldn't even say what I'm about to say. But if you're both what you claim, if you're both willing to do what must be done, then maybe you should know."

She paused for so long that Barnabas prompted her, "We should know what?"

"That was only the smallest part of what Huword did," she said quietly. Barnabas saw a flash of memory in her head: dead bodies and smoking ruins—and then she activated the door, stepped out, and was gone into the bustle of Gerris Station.

"Yes?" The senator sounded annoyed.

"I have a trace on the *Shinigami*." Norwun's ship shot through space. He was pushing the limits of its engines, but he knew he couldn't afford to slow. "It docked at Gerris

Station not too long ago. I was following what I thought was its trail, heading toward one of the Federation border stations, but they must have done that to confuse any pursuit. There are reports of a lockdown at the station."

"Good," the senator said. "Tell me when it's done—including the *Srisa*, and the assassin. I expect you to find the assassin."

They ended the call, and Norwun tried to calm down. He'd do this, he told himself. Others had failed to apprehend Barnabas because they'd underestimated his abilities. Norwun would not make the same mistake.

He pulled up the schematics of Gerris Station and set to work.

He had no idea where to begin searching for the assassin. All he could hope was that Barnabas would—and that he'd bargain for his life with the information.

CHAPTER FOURTEEN

"I'm telling you we should go *after her*," Shinigami argued again. She had brought her physical body into the conference room and had her arms crossed with impatience. She shook her head. "I don't know why you won't; it's not exactly a weird suggestion."

"She wanted us to find something," Barnabas argued back. "She said it wasn't hers to tell. And I know some of it, anyway. He killed a *lot* of people. I'd say he was a serial killer, but surely someone on his crew would have noticed that."

"If he did something bad—"

"He paid for it," Barnabas said flatly. "As far as she's concerned, the matter is closed."

"Yes, but it's *not* closed." Shinigami's rising frustration was clear. "He helped people, and we know who he helped. It was those fuckers in the Senate. He helped them while they were signing their people over to Koel Yennai."

"I know," Barnabas agreed.

"They didn't give a damn about their own citizens!"

"I know."

"Then why aren't you *doing* anything about it?" Shinigami exploded.

Once, this would have been the start of an argument between them, but they'd grown to know each other better now. Barnabas smiled at her.

"Shinigami, have you ever known me to stand by while injustice was done?"

"No." Shinigami sounded annoyed. "So I don't get why—"

"I've been debating the pros and cons of exposing the Jotun senators," Barnabas interrupted. "You saw what happened on Earth when Bethany Anne—well, you'll have heard about it, I imagine. The information was all there. People could see that their politicians were selfish and irresponsible, but the politicians lied through their teeth and some people bought it, then there were citizens arguing with one another about whether to forgive, and whether there *was* anything to forgive. If we go about this the wrong way, nothing changes." He sighed. "And it's not the Federation we're throwing into chaos. It's a government that isn't even ours."

Shinigami had fallen silent. Now she looked at Jeltor, whose biosuit was still as he listened to this.

"I can help," Barnabas told him. "I *will* help. Whatever you ask me to do, Jeltor, I'll trust your opinion. I can release the information we found about the bribes if you think it will do any good."

Jeltor considered this. "You're right to worry," he admitted. "I've seen senators hauled up for corruption charges before. They're always guilty—it's not like the charges are trumped up or anything—but the people who get charged are always just unlucky or out of favor with whoever's in power at the time. It robs the charges of their legitimacy, even though they *are* legitimate. People say, 'Well, everyone does it.'"

Barnabas nodded wearily. "Every species seems to do this. You know, I hoped that we'd get out here and other species would have the trick of forming ethical, workable governments. The more species we meet, however, the more I think corruption just goes hand in hand with sentience."

Shinigami looked annoyed. "Everything we do, someone comes along and undoes it the next moment. Nothing ever stays fixed."

"Nope." Barnabas was laughing, shaking his head as he agreed with her. "Nothing ever stays fixed."

"Then why are you *laughing*?" She came over to sit down and dropped her head onto her crossed arms. It was a delightfully theatrical gesture, and—as far as Barnabas could tell—something she *hadn't* learned from Bethany Anne or Tabitha.

It fascinated him to watch her display new mannerisms, from a snarky and relatively young AI to someone who fiercely valued her friends and was willing to learn new ways of interacting. When they had started working together, Barnabas had still been of the opinion that AI sentience wasn't true sentience.

He'd realized, over his time spent working with

Shinigami, just how wrong he had been. Her thoughts and emotions were as real as his own.

So he tried to comfort her now. "There's no point in being disappointed that things don't stay fixed, any more than there's a point in being disappointed that you have to keep weeding a garden or fix a house or a ship. God named us *stewards*, Shinigami, and stewards preserve what matters most to them. They tend to it."

She picked her head up. "I suppose if you're getting religious, you must be taking this at least a little bit seriously."

Barnabas shrugged. He had never quite adhered to any religion on Earth, but he still found value in many ways of conceptualizing God and the world. After seeing some of the religious disagreements that unfolded on Earth, however, he did not speak of his faith except among close friends—and often, not even then.

"I *am* taking it seriously," he assured her. "I simply want to make sure that, whatever I do, it actually brings *Justice* to these senators instead of them just getting off the hook."

"And whatever they were doing," Jeltor said, bringing it back around, "it sounds like Huword was caught up in it. I *wish* I knew who had him assassinated. I feel like if we could jump ahead to knowing what they know, we'd be able to make more progress."

"Exactly!" Shinigami made a satisfied noise. "See?" she asked Barnabas. "I'm not the only one who thinks that."

"I know you're not," Barnabas said patiently, "but I think it's important to go through the process. It's not as if the assassin tossed a coin and decided not to tell us. She had a *reason*. We don't know what it was yet."

Shinigami was still grumbling when she perked up and

turned her head as though she were listening. It was such a human gesture that Barnabas also looked around, trying to catch any faint sound she might have noticed. Then he realized that she was probably "hearing" through some of her other sensors.

"There's a maintenance problem," she said slowly. "Maybe? There are some people trapped in a room on the other side of the station."

Barnabas and Jeltor looked at one another. Shinigami was still staring into space, frowning in concentration as she worked her way through the station reports like a human would. She didn't waste processing power on emoting while she was thinking about other things.

"Something about—a new Jotun ship that docked." She sat up straighter and looked right at Barnabas. "Not too long ago. And now there are people trapped in some chamber and station alerts are being sent."

Barnabas was out of the room so fast he practically climbed over the table. He sprinted down the hallways to his rooms, unbuttoning his formal shirt and vest as he went, and got into his armor in record time before sprinting back out—only to immediately collide with Jeltor.

Jeltor made a surprised noise and Barnabas gave a muffled grunt of pain. Running high-speed into spiky metal *hurt*.

"Where are you going?" Jeltor asked.

"They're here," Barnabas said grimly. "The Senate sent someone, and I'll be damned if I let this one self-destruct too."

"I'm coming with you," Jeltor stated at once. When Barnabas made for the airlock, he followed.

"No." Barnabas shook his head. "There's something more to this. We must be very careful. Here's what I want *you* to do..."

In the control room of the *Ur'talis*, Norwun made a slight adjustment to one system and closed off another.

The station administrator was fighting back. He didn't know what he was fighting *against*, of course, but he was running through all the diagnostic checks he could think of to get civilians out of that part of the station.

Norwun had chosen his location well, however. This part of the station had once been used to house diplomats and other high-value visitors, so it ran on different circuits than the rest of the station. That had been intended to save the diplomats if someone tried to destroy the entire station to get to them.

Now it would help Norwun keep his captives in place while he summoned Barnabas to play rescuer.

It was both a good and bad time to have tried this, he was finding out. Every ship at Gerris Station had been trapped here for days, which had wreaked havoc across the entire sector regarding travel and trade.

In a desperate bid to fix the problem, the administrator had deployed every maintenance worker he had to find the cause of the ship lock. He hadn't found it, of course, but they were all a lot more knowledgeable about the station than they had been even a few days ago.

On the other hand, they were all tired and overworked, and Norwun was fairly sure he could keep them from breaking his hold on this part of the station—at least until he'd dealt with Barnabas.

The door opened behind him, and one of his team members came in.

"It's done," she told Norwun. Reqara was older than the rest of his team. Her body was a rare pink color and she was much smaller than most Jotuns, but it would be foolish to underestimate her because of her size as many did. She was competent and deadly, and she had learned the trick of behaving in a way that didn't attract attention.

She was the one who had set up a special surprise for Barnabas. Now she came to stand by the control panels.

"How long will it be until he comes, do you think?"

"Not long," Norwun predicted. "He can't resist getting involved when there are innocent people to save." He swiveled in his tank to look at her. "It doesn't bother you, does it?"

"It would bother me if you did it any other way," she said bluntly. "He's dangerous. Better to set up a trap than try to face him 'honorably' and lose." Her voice showed the depths of her contempt. "Like everyone else did."

Norwun nodded and settled down to wait.

It wouldn't be long. He could tell.

Biset's biosuit stood motionless in the corner as he swam idly around his tank. At the edge of the tank there were a few small fish that were huddled among the plants, hoping he hadn't noticed them. He would hunt them later; the thought made him shiver in anticipation.

Jotuns were more civilized now. They liked to wear biosuits and be fed via small particles in their tanks—and in most cases, this was good. Biset could hardly argue with the progress the Jotuns had made since they had perfected biosuit technology.

But it was good to remember what you were. The Jotuns weren't simply aquatic creatures who had to use machines to give them strength. They were hunters.

Before he hunted, however, he had to make sure his operatives were on the right track. A set of video screens in his tank showed information from Gerris Station, where Norwun's ship had recently docked.

Biset could admit he'd had doubts. Many otherwise-logical people of many species had underestimated Barnabas and wound up dead. They seemed to want to face him one-on-one in combat for some reason.

Their funeral, not his—until it came to this particular mission. Now he had a vested interest in making sure Norwun did things sensibly, and he was pleased to see that the operative was setting everything up just like he'd said he would.

Barnabas would be so distracted by the choice Norwun had given him that he would fall right into the trap before he had time to notice it was there.

And Biset would be the hero of the Senate. No one would know, of course; Biset could not afford to advertise that he was the one who'd ordered this. It was a pity. They'd all owe him favors if they knew.

They'd owe him, he thought, whether they realized it or not. He'd collect someday.

For now, he'd focus on what mattered: eliminating the threat.

CHAPTER FIFTEEN

A crowd of people had gathered near the entrance to the locked section of the station. Part of the group was, understandably, maintenance workers, station staff, police, and media. Barnabas had to duck under multiple sets of broadcast equipment, and, in one case, nearly ended up oversetting a food cart in his attempt to stay out of the shot.

Why are you bothering? Shinigami asked him. *The media are such pricks.*

In this case, there's a reasonable public interest. If they want to endanger their lives to get a good backdrop for their story—and they don't interfere with the rescue teams—I'm not going to stop them. It's the rest *of these clowns I want to strangle. Who hears that there's a malfunction on a space station and goes there to check it out? Any reasonable person would go the other way.*

You've met people before, right? They're dumb.

I wish I could refute that.

Barnabas spotted Westo Gor'rathi, the station administrator, speaking with some of the maintenance workers, and headed that way. He had buttoned his jacket so that his weaponry was not immediately obvious. For all he knew, this was simply an equipment malfunction.

He highly doubted it, however.

He waited until the administrator dispatched the group he was speaking with, sending all of them running in various directions to check certain things. Barnabas was impressed with the male's competence. Although harried, the Torcellan seemed to have a good handle on what was going on, and he was decisive in his orders.

When he turned and saw Barnabas, his eyes narrowed slightly. "Mr. Nacht." He sounded slightly uncertain of the title.

Barnabas decided it was as good as any. He wasn't going to waste time on corrections on vampire naming conventions when there were more pressing issues. "Mr. Gor'rathi. Thank you for allowing my ship to dock."

"I notice that the ship lock has not yet been lifted," Gor'rathi stated somewhat acidly, "and that there was a gun battle near the loading docks as soon as you landed."

"We're working on it—and the term 'battle' is quite an exaggeration, I assure you. The sole bullet in that incident went into my ship, and we resolved the matter without any further violence or harm to the station or bystanders."

Gor'rathi's eyes narrowed further. "Are you a lawyer?"

"I am not." Barnabas tried to keep a touch of annoyance out of his tone. "Mr. Gor'rathi, may I perhaps be of assistance in this matter?" He nodded toward the locked doors.

Gor'rathi studied him for a long moment. "Now, why would you think you could be of use, I wonder?"

Barnabas returned his half-smile, aware that his eyes were not exactly friendly. "Call it a hunch," he said smoothly. "I don't think this is random, although I'm not presently at liberty to say why." In the spirit of fairness, he added, "I'd be happy to be proven wrong."

"Unfortunately, I cannot make you happy." Gor'rathi folded his hands in front of him and gave a world-weary sigh. He glanced at the media, who were all giving him hopeful looks, and made an effort to keep his face calm.

Pale and well-dressed, he nonetheless flouted Torcellan custom by wearing his hair in a single neat braid down his back. There were no decorations in it that Barnabas could see. It was a curious choice.

Now he looked at Barnabas, black eyes watchful. His voice was very low as he said, "We received a message just before you arrived. It noted that you would be along shortly and we should send you in alone or they will kill the civilians in the section. We asked for more information, but none came."

I should have known.

You did *know. It's why you're wearing your armor.*

He had to admit she was onto something there. Barnabas looked at the assembled media.

"I suggest you tell them I'm a maintenance worker."

"I have experience dealing with the media, Mr. Nacht."

Shinigami was snickering in Barnabas' head. *I can picture this guy calling Bethany Anne "Ms. Nacht."*

She only gets upset at intentional rudeness, Barnabas pointed out.

Still funny. Empress. Many-clawed murder machine. Bloody armor and a team of Bitches. "Ms. Nacht."

Barnabas refrained from rolling his eyes. "I'll go in, then," he told the Torcellan.

"Before you do, so that I can prepare myself..." Gor'rathi looked resigned. "What are the odds there will be deaths?"

Barnabas gave a very wide smile and let his teeth lengthen slightly. "That depends on whether the person doing this is present."

He left, Gor'rathi staring open-mouthed after him.

You have a flair for theatrics, you know, Shinigami observed.

I have no idea what you mean. Barnabas approached the doors. *How do you think they're going to let me in without letting any of the rest of them out?*

Oh, that I can tell you. They were all ordered into a separate locked room.

And you're getting a fix on who they are and how they're doing this, right?

Do I look like I just fell off the turnip truck?

Well...

RUDE. You never *insult a lady's looks.*

It's your mind, Barnabas pointed out, *and in this case, the lady walked right into it. Also, since when have you ever been ladylike?*

Shinigami was still presumably trying to come up with an answer when the doors slid open, and a voice said over the loudspeaker, "Hello, Barnabas."

"Hello." Barnabas stepped through the door as if he weren't aware of the media crowding forward to get a last shot. *Any progress?*

No, she said glumly. *I don't like dresses or doing my hair or not swearing or—*

I meant on figuring out how he has the doors locked down.

Oh. Yeah, I did get that. Let me know when you want me to let you all out.

Excellent. Time to go hunting. Barnabas let himself smile as he walked down the hallway. It was very quiet until he got far enough to hear the muffled yelling from one of the rooms ahead.

"Why am I here?" he asked conversationally.

"I think you know exactly why you're here," the voice responded. "You're sticking your nose where it doesn't belong."

"So you're locking a bunch of civilians inside a section of the station because... Help me out, here."

"Would you have come if we'd asked to meet with you?"

"Probably." Barnabas stopped in front of a room and peered inside. Several aliens were beating on the walls and door, and their efforts redoubled when they saw him.

His opponent seemed surprised. "Interesting, but irrelevant. You have a nasty habit of killing people."

"Only when they try to kill someone else first," Barnabas said. He was unsurprised when the door opened to let him in. A sharp command from their captor kept the other people away from the door, and they stared at Barnabas in open mistrust as the door closed behind him.

He nodded pleasantly to them.

"All right," he said, talking to the speakers he could see on the wall. "I'm here. Now what?"

His opponent didn't answer him. He didn't need to. The captives scattered, parting before Barnabas as if they'd been blown away by wind, and Barnabas saw a large object in the corner.

Of course, there's a bomb. Why am I surprised?

Because you don't have a direct feed into the surveillance cameras? I found it a couple of minutes ago. If you can drop a bot near it without him seeing, I can defuse it. You'll have to work on it without working on it, if you see my meaning, so he doesn't get the sense we're making any progress.

Fair enough. Barnabas heaved a sigh and walked over to where the bomb was now ticking down a count in large red letters. *It's like a giant roomful of clichés. They're a James Bond villain.* He looked up at a nearby camera. "I take it you expect me to defuse this?"

No, Mr. Nacht, I expect you to die, Shinigami said in a surprisingly good impression of Goldfinger.

Barnabas' lips twitched. *All right, that was a good one.*

"You can certainly try, though." The voice sounded amused. "But you won't get very far. Only I can defuse the bomb...which I will do if our conversation goes satisfactorily."

He's lying out his ass.

Yes, thank you, I knew that. Although that's not the phrasing I would have used.

Yeah, well, what do you know? You've still got a stick up yours.

Barnabas knelt by the bomb and looked over the casing carefully. Out of the corner of his eye, he noted where the cameras were around the room, and shifted subtly to allow a bot to drop from his cuff to the floor. It scurried under the bomb and was soon lost in the internal workings.

It had been Shinigami who'd suggested the cuff compartments, pointing out that people often needed to deploy small machines on the sly. The compartments had a catch hidden on the sleeves of the jacket so that Barnabas could pretend to scratch his arm, and the bots had been programmed to move only after he shifted his hand in a particular way.

He was fond of the system. Every operative of any sort had their favorite gadgets, and while he was fond of the classics— knives, guns, and teeth—he was also beginning to enjoy the bots. It was immensely satisfying to talk in circles with his enemies, knowing that all the while, little bots were crawling through their systems.

He pressed a button and noticed a very faint slowness in his muscles. No one else would have noticed it, but he did. Alarmed, he checked for any signs of poison in the air but found none.

Shinigami, something's wrong.

I don't see anyth— Oh, hell. He's venting the room. Very slowly. And I'm delighted to tell you that this means I won't be able to open those blast doors until we resolve the problem if there's a pressure differential above 3pa.

That's an insanely sensitive system.

Focus on the big picture, boss. You have an air leak. Pretend you don't notice for now; I'll fix it. Just keep him distracted.

I'll do what I can, Barnabas replied. He looked around. "What do you want to talk about?" he asked his mysterious captor. He did not have to feign impatience. This was all a farce; they had no intention of letting anyone in this room go.

But he just had to play along for a little bit, while Gar, Jeltor, and Shinigami enacted the rest of the plan.

"Tafa! Gar! Thank the gods I found you." Jeltor hurried over, his suit clanking.

"Hello, Jeltor." Tafa waved. "Uh-oh, that's not a happy face."

"How can you *tell*?" Gar asked plaintively.

"Don't give away our secrets," Jeltor told Tafa. "It's so much fun trying to watch people guess."

She giggled. Tafa and Jeltor had first met while being held hostage by a mercenary group, so they had first spent time together with the fear of death hanging over everything they did. It was nice to be in a situation that wasn't quite so grim.

Although this one was getting there.

"Listen," Jeltor said, "Shinigami is tracing some signals, and we'll need to go to a specific dock and board a ship."

"Oh?" Gar looked worried. "What's wrong?"

"Someone's taken hostages," Jeltor explained. Tafa drew in her breath sharply, and he nodded. "Barnabas and Shinigami have a plan. He's the distraction, and you and I will go attack the ship that's sending the signals. They aren't soldiers, apparently. They locked the section down remotely."

Gar looked pleased. "And we're going to go pay them a visit?"

"Yes. Yes, we are." Jeltor sounded just as pleased as Gar looked. "Well, probably not Tafa."

"Oh, good." Tafa's shoulders slumped in relief. "I'll go back to the ship?" She looked at them fiercely. "And be *safe.*"

"We will," Jeltor assured her. "Oh, and one more thing—don't mention to my wife where I went, will you? If she finds out I went charging off to do this, I'll be lucky to get out of it alive."

CHAPTER SIXTEEN

Barnabas' unseen captor wasted no time beginning their interrogation. Barnabas guessed it was a Jotun simply because of the known players in the situation, but as with many Jotuns, he was not able to determine whether they were male or female.

"How did you learn what happened on the *Srisa?*" they asked him now.

"We intercepted the distress call." Barnabas had decided to behave as though he were beginning to feel the effects of his fatigue, but also as if he had not yet realized what was going on. He paused at his pretended work of defusing the bomb and acted as though he were trying to catch his breath.

He didn't have to look far for inspiration. The rest of the prisoners in the room were starting to move more slowly, and Barnabas caught some of them yawning.

"How coincidental," his captor suggested smoothly. "You just happened to be in the right place at the right time —and be the first one to get to that ship."

"I...wasn't."

Good, Shinigami commented. *Little pauses. That's good. He probably knows you have a good amount of built-in resistance. If you can make him think it's happening slowly, he'll stay engaged.*

I want to make sure you remember that the rest of the people in this room don't *have any built-in resistance.*

Oh, I remember, don't worry. I'm working on something.

There would be no speeding her up, Barnabas knew. He also knew that she was working faster than anyone else could. He could not imagine how much data she had sifted through to find out who this person was.

"You weren't what?" the Jotun asked.

"What?"

Now the Jotun sounded annoyed. "I said you were the first one to the ship and you said—ah. Who was there before you?"

"I don't know." Barnabas paused, pretending to focus on breathing for a few moments. "We saw wreckage. There was a ship that shot at us."

"What happened to that ship?" The voice had shifted. It was melodious now. Persuasive.

Barnabas' mind raced. This Jotun had noticed the missing ship but did not know *why* it was missing. That gave him a little bit of wiggle room to play with their head.

"They said...uh..." He rubbed his forehead.

"You spoke to them?" The voice was sharp with surprise.

Barnabas looked up at the camera as if remembering to be angry. Some of the people had laid down to sleep, and the rest were sitting in a daze. It was easy to mimic their mannerisms, although he was beginning to worry that Shinigami, used to the more robust systems of her friends, would not restore air quickly enough for these people.

That was just him worrying because he was helpless, he realized. He wanted to be at the forefront of this mission, striking out at something.

And this person, whoever they were, was making sure he could not do so. He had to admit that was clever.

He could be clever too, though. "Did you think I would shoot down a ship without speaking to the pilot?" he demanded. "Of course I did. We cornered them. That ship wasn't as fast as the *Shinigami*."

"And what did they tell you?" demanded his captor.

Shinigami, I'm running out of ways to pretend to defuse this thing. I've been fiddling with one screw for the past thirty seconds.

Yeah, I noticed that. I'm pretty sure it plays into the oxygen deprivation thing, at least.

There's that.

Hang on just for a few more minutes, No one's getting brain damage, I promise.

Right. I'll do what I can. How are things with Gar?

Very, very good. I'll show you video after this.

Barnabas hid a smile and tried to decide what would most unsettle this person to hear but not cause them to blow the station up immediately. A sudden stroke of inspiration came to him. He'd been a thorn in the side of the Jotun government so far, but he was just one human on one ship. If he wanted them to hold off, he needed them to think there was a much bigger threat for them to worry about.

And what was a bigger threat to a government than another government? He had seen alien bodies in the assassin's thoughts. It wasn't out of the question that another government would know of Huword and hire a Jotun to assassinate him. For all he knew, that *was* what had happened.

"They told me something *very* interesting." He slurred his words a bit, still pretending to be out of air, but he smiled at the cameras. "Seems there's another government interested in this wrongdoing."

"What?"

"Yes. There was another ship they couldn't shoot down, a ship they thought *we* were affiliated with."

"A human ship."

"That was the thing; they didn't know. They just said they knew the look of black ops. You have that term out here, right? The sort of thing the government doesn't want anyone to know about?"

Whoa, there, Hoss, you're getting animated as the oxygen comes back.

Oh, is it back? How'd you manage that?

I just had to get a set of signals going to his ship so he'd think he was still sucking the air out. He doesn't have accurate diagnostics on the station anymore, and the signals he's sending aren't going anywhere.

And?

And what?

And the bomb, *Shinigami?*

Oh, that's also fixed.

So...do we need to keep this charade up anymore?

Actually, yes. Just for a few moments more.

Barnabas bit back a sigh. His opponent hadn't said anything further, and he was intrigued to think what might be going on in their head.

"Hello? Are you looking up 'black ops?' Because I wasn't lying about what it meant."

Black ops. Biset's surprise caused him to jet backward in his tank. He righted himself and shook with worry, his tentacles churning the water. Nearby, the fish huddled in their plants, gone absolutely still at this new threat.

Black ops. Someone knew. A *government* knew.

They knew enough to eliminate Huword but they hadn't come after the committee yet, and what the hell did that mean? Where was that ship coming next?

To Jotuna, that was where. Biset knew it. Sooner or later, every part of this was going to come out—and not in the way it was supposed to. Not with armies and fleets under the command of the committee, but instead with trade wars and sanctions and accusations.

His fury swept the waters into a storm, sending ink and heat radiating from him as he thrashed and raged. He arrowed down to the corner of the tank and grabbed one of the fish, electrocuting it and tearing it to pieces with his tentacles. The fish struggled, the others fled, and he felt a savage sense of satisfaction as he hunted them down and destroyed them.

When it was over, the tank was filled with blood and random scales, and Biset knew he should be satisfied.

But he was not.

He needed to find the source of this disturbance, and find it soon.

The question was, should Biset let Norwun chase down the truth...or should he call in someone else and tie up that loose end?

The human was still moving slowly, slurring his words. He was getting ready—although he didn't know it—to die.

Norwun couldn't take any pleasure in that anymore.

Black ops. He knew the term; every government had its version. *He* was black ops, and had been for most of his career. The things he had done would shock the average Jotun to their very core. What had happened to Huword was child's play. Norwun did worse pretty much weekly.

And now some other government, a government they could not even guess at—although it didn't seem to be human—knew what was going on and had sent their people. Whoever the assassin was, the ship had picked them up and was long gone, and the Jotun government was still none the wiser as to what was happening here.

Norwun had a sudden memory of the senator and their worry. They feared that *something* would be uncovered, and Norwun had no doubts about what would happen to him if he failed to keep it hidden.

That was why they'd sent him to the *Srisa*—to figure out who'd killed Huword and why, and eliminate all witnesses.

Right now, Norwun was failing at that objective.

He'd known some of what Huword was—a spy who for years had fed information to the Senate about the mutinous rumblings in the Navy. Any number of issues had been quietly averted, the instigators promoted or shamed or put in the way of convenient missiles. That would have been enough to earn Huword's death.

If this were a rival government, though, then Huword had been involved in something *much* more important.

Norwun fought the urge to send a message to his contact: You should have told me how much was at stake.

He didn't. He didn't have a death wish, after all, and sending that message would be asking to have his ship put on self-destruct. He knew his employers had ways to do that. There were probably failsafes in his suit as well, no matter how carefully he'd tried to keep himself free of them.

Now he had to figure out which government it was and what they knew, and take out anyone who could report on the information.

Step one was taking out Barnabas. He wasn't important anymore. Norwun pressed a single button to detonate the bomb. Let the station try to figure out who'd done it; all trace of his ship was gone from their systems.

Nothing happened, however. Barnabas was looking around.

"Hellooooo?" The human waved his arms. "Anybody there?"

He was getting loopy, which Norwun would normally have enjoyed seeing but could only snarl at now. Loopy was not *dead*, and Barnabas very much needed to be dead.

Norwun pressed the button again. And again. And again. Why wasn't it *working*?

The door slid open behind him, and he turned to tell

Reqara to finish this herself. It wasn't Reqara, however. It was, of all ridiculous things, an armored Luvendi. Norwun would have laughed if the ridiculous thing hadn't been pointing a gun directly at his head.

"Talk, asshole," it said.

CHAPTER SEVENTEEN

Air pressure is stable, Shinigami reported, *and...doors open. Gar and Jeltor are questioning our Jotun friend. All is well, but you should probably join them.*

On my way. Barnabas turned on his heel and ran for the door.

Almost as soon as they knew a Jotun ship had docked, that same ship had managed to get into the station's data and wipe any trace of itself. They hadn't been able to figure out what bay it was docked at or any more specifics on it.

Shinigami and Barnabas had known that the ship's interactions with Barnabas would allow them to trace signals directly back to the ship, and so Barnabas had gone in as a distraction. At the time, of course, they'd been expecting to find hordes of mercenaries.

Gar and Jeltor, meanwhile, had gone to the ship once Shinigami found it and snuck on board to figure out who and what they were dealing with. Between Gar's unexpected skills in combat and Jeltor's knowledge of the Jotun government, Barnabas was sure they could get anything they needed out of the crew.

But he hadn't gotten this far in life by expecting things to go *well,* and he was going to be ready for complications until every member of that crew was restrained or verifiably, indisputably dead.

And then, given the self-destruct on that other government ship, he was going to expect some more complications.

Heads up—you'll have company in a few. Shinigami sounded halfway between amused and impressed. *Gor'rathi is sending soldiers in. I restored his access to the video feeds so he can see that people aren't hurt, but he's cautious. You may have trouble getting out.*

Tell him to send medics. Never mind, I'll do it. Barnabas could hear the guards, and the next corner he skidded around, he saw the force. Composed of many different species, the group nonetheless had similar uniforms of blue and white that fit everyone well, and a set of weapons that looked unusually useful.

Many of those weapons came up at once. The guards seemed to view his high speed as suspicious, and Barnabas knew better than to run headlong into bullets.

"The bomb is defused, and all of the trapped people are safe." He pointed back down the hallway. "The ship that was causing the problems has been neutralized and will not be able to harm any more systems, but I *do* need to go deal with the crew."

There was the faint buzz of earpieces, and a few of them bent their heads to listen.

"Mr. Gor'rathi wants you to bring the criminals to the station jail," one of the guards said.

"I'll do that." Barnabas doubted the people in question would survive long enough to be brought there, but he kept that to himself. He edged around the group, pointing them down the hall to the roomful of former captives, and took off again.

In the station, he was greeted with cheers. Aliens rushed forward to grab his hands and his coat, and Barnabas had to fight to extricate himself without throwing anyone across the room—and with *his* strength, he certainly could if he wasn't careful.

God bless it, get them off me!

Nah, this is fun to watch. Besides, Gar and Jeltor are holding their own just fine.

"Holding their own?" *Does that mean there's a fight?*

No. Well, yes. Don't worry about it, though. They'll do just fine until you get there.

Son of a bitch, Barnabas swore. He managed to pry himself out of the arms of a female Torcellan who was trying to kiss his cheek—or, at least, he *hoped* that was what she was trying to kiss—and took special care to unwrap a Luvendi's fingers from his wrist, but by then, several more aliens had joined the throng. "I'll, ah, I'll be right back, I promise. I just have one more thing to do—"

Shinigami was laughing delightedly in his head.

Don't laugh! This is a problem!

It's not a problem; it's just—oh. Oh, it is a problem.

Barnabas froze. *What? What happened?*

Get to Bay 52. Right now. Shinigami's worry was palpable. *They've called in reinforcements.*

Barnabas stopped trying to be polite. "Everybody back!"

At his bellow, the crowd stopped in its tracks. People scattered away from him and he gave a little sigh of relief before taking off at high speed for Bay 52.

Hang on, Gar, I'm coming.

His worry tripled when Gar, who was normally full of pride in his fighting abilities and ready to take on the world alone, responded only, *Good.*

The fight had started well. Shinigami had gotten the doors of the Jotun ship open without them having the first idea about it.

And what a ship it was. If they hadn't been trying to be stealthy, Gar would have whistled in amazement. As it was, he shook his head in silent awe, and even Jeltor looked impressed. If any ship could have given the *Shinigami* a run for its money—and a lot of ships had tried and failed spectacularly at that—it might be this one.

It was a frigate-class ship, clearly made for atmosphere as well as space, but there the similarities ended. The *Shinigami* was sleek and shining, painted beautifully and clearly state of the art. This ship looked old and battered, so much so that the casual observer probably wouldn't be able to tell just how dangerous it was.

But if they knew anything about ships, the observer would know to be very, very careful of this one. Its shape showed the sleek lines of excellent craftsmanship, and the scars on it were bad enough that the ship should be in several pieces. The fact that it wasn't was a very bad sign.

The amount of venting on the back suggested that the engines could burn harder than almost any Gar had seen. They belonged on a much larger ship, as did the missile bays. This ship was armed to the teeth, and it was *fast*.

Still, the lack of alarm showed that Shinigami had gotten into their systems with them none the wiser.

Gar and Jeltor crept aboard, weapons drawn. Gar went first, given that his species offered him the element of surprise in pretty much any combat encounter. Enemies tended to laugh themselves sick when they saw him in armor, which he hated. He had to admit it was a good distraction, though.

He made them sorry for it, too. He was Luvendi, yes, but it turned out that with reinforcement of the bone structure and training from Barnabas, a Luvendi could be exceedingly dangerous. Gar could hit hard enough to break the bones of most other species.

Most. He had yet to fight a Brakalon in hand-to-hand combat, and he wasn't looking forward to the experience. But with Barnabas, you could be fairly sure that it would come at some point.

Shinigami said into his mind, and Jeltor's suit, that the person sending the signals was in a control room at the center of the ship. She couldn't sense any other signals aboard, and only one Jotun had gotten off the ship.

The doors slid open as the Jotun was speaking to someone—Barnabas, Gar expected. He could see the familiar shape on the Jotun's screens.

"Hellooooo?" Barnabas was saying, waving his arms.

Tell Barnabas he looks ridiculous, Gar told Shinigami.

You have mental speech. Tell him yourself.

I'm too scared to do that. Barnabas would demand a sparring match, wipe the floor with him, and then ask if he'd learned his lesson about manners. Then he'd probably demand a rematch. Then, if he still didn't think Gar had learned his lesson, there would be push-ups. Luvendi were *not* suited to push-ups. Gar hadn't even known what they were until he'd met Tabitha, who had told him that they were a wager and punishment metric among the Rangers and Bitches.

He could believe it.

Right now, though, he had more pressing concerns. Gar strode across the room and, as the Jotun turned to look at him, Gar brought his Jean Dukes out to point directly at the thing's tank.

"Talk, asshole," he said.

You're starting to fit in, Shinigami commented.

Thanks that means a lot. Gar smiled. "You aren't talking," he added to the Jotun. "Who the fuck are you? Start there."

The Jotun looked at Jeltor and then back at Gar as if to see whether Gar was still there. While the biosuits didn't show faces, Gar could tell from the speed of movement that disbelief was the primary emotion right now.

And then the Jotun's arm shot out at an angle that wouldn't be possible on most species and grabbed the barrel of Gar's gun, dragging it sideways.

Gar took two steps along with the motion, and when the Jotun would think he was having success, Gar planted his feet and wrenched back in the other direction. Metal screamed in the biosuit, and the Jotun made an involuntary sound of surprise.

"Yeah," Gar said savagely, "it's like *that.*" Still holding the gun with one hand, he let go with the other to level a punch at the Jotun's ocular display.

Jeltor had told him that one of the best things you could do in this situation was to take out the various sensory apparatus, leaving the Jotun to "see" from inside the tank with its more limited biological eyes and ears. The combination of water and air would cause the Jotun to misjudge distances, and being disoriented was never a good thing in a fight.

The Jotun knew what Gar was trying to do. It gave a yell and punched back while shaking the barrel of the gun as hard as it could to try to make Gar let go of it.

"Fuck off!" Gar yelled. "You can't even shoot this gun! I said, get off! Jeltor—"

"We have company!" Jeltor yelled back. There was clanking in the hallway outside. "The son of a bitch called for help."

"There wasn't anyone else on the ship! Shinigami said—"

I didn't think there was! Shinigami sounded almost panicked. *I'm still not seeing them. Are you* sure *that—*

The door burst open, and four more Jotuns stood there, arms up to show the embedded rifles.

"Pretty damned sure, yeah!" Gar yelled.

Shit. I'm calling Barnabas in.

That sounds like a good idea!

Gar watched for a moment as Jeltor swung into action, leveling a flamethrower at the other Jotun, who swung their arms away for fear of the metal melting.

Gar didn't waste any time. It was five against two, and the Jotuns were trained to fight hand-to-hand. He had to quickly even the odds. He brought his leg up over the back of the Jotun's chair and bashed his knee into the head of the biosuit. The jolt that went through him hurt like hell, but he repressed the old instincts that told him to back down and plead for mercy.

Once, he'd had to think his way out of every situation. Now, if his thinking brought him to the conclusion that taking everyone down was the best way to go about things, he could do that instead of having to bargain and beg.

He'd sworn a vow that he was never going to beg again.

The Jotun staggered, but because it was in a biosuit and not a biological body, it didn't let go of the gun like Gar had hoped it would.

He would take down the array first, then worry about maybe severing some of the connections to the limbs. Gar ignored the pain as he brought his knee up repeatedly, bashing it into the Jotun's input and output array until the thing began to stagger, clearly disoriented and blind.

He'd have taken the whole thing down and finished it except for the yell he heard. Jeltor was being swarmed by the other four, who had knives and needles sliding out of compartments in their suits. Gar had seen the pictures of Huword's body, so he knew what was coming next.

Fury filled him, and he threw himself into the fray with a scream of rage.

CHAPTER EIGHTEEN

Barnabas sprinted through the station with the yells fading behind him. A few people looked at him askance and were clearly marking what he wore, ready to tell station security about him if he should later turn out to be a criminal.

No one tried to stop him, though. The bigger the station, the fewer people tended to get involved in events like this. No one was going to ask too many questions, or— God forbid—put themselves in danger.

Barnabas ground his teeth at their self-serving cowardice and was somewhat comforted that it was working in his favor right now.

Bay 52 was at the far end of one of the corridors, and he could hear the fight between his teammates and the Jotun black ops crew from about halfway down. Yells and clanks were emanating from the open door of the ship, along with a few crashes.

Any special skills I should know about in these people?

Nothing, in particular, Shinigami reported. *Knives. Well, there are needles. I'm not sure how ready they are to mess with a human, though.*

Let's not test it.

Agreed. She paused. *I think you might have worried them more than you intended with that lie about the black ops ship.*

I couldn't let them think they'd gotten everything out of me—

No, I know why you did it. If they thought everyone who knew about Huword was on this station, they'd have tried to blow the whole thing. I get that. But I think you might have stumbled upon something.

Something like? Up the gangway he went, opening his coat and pulling out his Jean Dukes Specials. Teeth weren't useful against biosuits, after all.

I don't know. The way he responded to what you said, though, and what the assassin had already said about Huword? Together, that makes me think maybe Huword really was involved in something that other governments might not like.

So, an equal-opportunity asshole, fucking over Jotuns and aliens indiscriminately?

That's the one. Take a left here. Yep. There you go.

The fight was much more of a brawl than anything precise. In the background, Barnabas could see a Jotun staggering around in circles, trying to orient itself despite a crushed sensory array, and in the foreground...

Barnabas slid into the fray with deadly grace. He holstered his pistols, and his hands came up to grab at two open slots on the Jotun's suit. He had to double-check to make sure it wasn't Jeltor.

In the future, he decided, Jeltor would have to wear something distinctive. Maybe war paint. Or a hat.

The thought of Jeltor in a party hat made him snort

with laughter as he dragged the other Jotun off-balance and threw it back into a wall. Nearby, Gar was trying to take on two at once, and Jeltor was engaged in a battle of flamethrowers with a Jotun whose jellyfish body was unusually small and a pink color Barnabas hadn't seen before. Most of the Jotun he'd seen were shades of purple.

His opponent swung the head of its biosuit to look at him, and Barnabas felt a certain malevolence in its actions.

Well, if it wasn't happy about this, it could have avoided the situation by not putting civilians in the crossfire.

"Are you the one who came up with that stupid plan?" Barnabas asked it. As it tried to struggle upright, he took two steps and kicked his back leg out, sending it reeling back once more. There was a clank and the sound of something breaking this time when it hit the wall.

Good.

"You're the one who's been interfering," it hissed at him. "And you're going to learn not to do that."

"I don't think I am." Barnabas flipped out his Jean Dukes and blew the thing to bits. Its tank had exploded, along with the Jotun body inside it, and as he watched, the whole apparatus went dark and thudded to its knees.

In the sudden silence, Barnabas looked around to find the rest of the group staring at him open-mouthed. He felt a pang of sadness for Jeltor—it was never good to see one of your species brutally killed—but otherwise, he could only feel satisfaction.

"I don't like you," he told the remaining four, including the disoriented one who had frozen at the sound of the gunshot. "I don't like anyone who decides to use civilians as tools. If you have a problem with me, it's because you're doing things I will not abide. You could have cleared that up at *any* time."

They didn't answer, only swung into action once more. The pink Jotun whipped out one arm and loosed a stream of bullets at Barnabas—or at the place he'd been standing when its arm started moving.

He joined Gar in the center of the fight with the other two. If the pink one wanted to keep shooting, it was going to have to take the chance of shooting its compatriots. A moment later, the use of flamethrowers and knives let him know that it wasn't willing to do so and it had returned to its fight with Jeltor.

These two had their needles out, apparently ready to do as much damage as possible to the biological bodies they were fighting. The needles were short, capped with what Barnabas guessed was a water-soluble plug that would dissolve and let the contents out as soon as it was in a creature's bloodstream. The needle was too short for him to bend it, and he couldn't tell if it would go through his armor. Jean Dukes would be deeply offended even by the suggestion, but Jellyfish Sector had a lot of technology the Etheric Empire had never run into before.

So, with no other options that he could think of, Barnabas settled for ripping the suit's arm off.

It wasn't exactly easy—the suits were made to be durable—but it was *very* satisfying. It came off with the clatter of screws and shattered bits of metal, and the pops of various tubes and wires shearing loose.

Barnabas and the Jotun stared at one another for a moment—the Jotun shocked and Barnabas very pleased with himself—before Barnabas started beating it with its own arm. Gar was almost laughing too hard to do the same to his opponent, but only almost. A similar set of screeches came soon after, followed by a pleased chortle from Gar and an unintelligible yell from one of the Jotuns.

"We still haven't gotten them to talk!" he called to Barnabas.

"Oh, right." Barnabas wound up and backhanded his Jotun with its own hand. "You know, I'm not sure I care anymore. They're going to die, and we'll figure out what we need to know from someone else. *Like the other black ops team,*" he added at the top of his lungs.

At the side of the room, the Jotun who'd been staggering back and forth betrayed a sudden interest.

That was probably the one he'd been talking to, then.

"I don't suppose you'd have any guesses as to which government sent them," Barnabas called.

What's your plan here? Shinigami asked skeptically. *There is no black ops team. They don't exist.*

Yeah, but think for a moment. If I stumbled on one of their fears, they probably have a good idea of who'd be angry—of who would send a team.

Ohhhh, you're sneaky. This is the beer competition all over again—throw out false info and see who nibbles.

Great. Barnabas threw the arm away and punched his Jotun in the tank as hard as he could. The material of the tank creaked, and the Jotun fluttered around in distress. *Now I want a beer.*

Better than your juice obsession.

And now I want juice.

You're very suggestible, you know that? It's a good thing you never discovered infomercials.

I did. Barnabas swept the leg or tried to. *I have seven Wonder Mops,* he told Shinigami as he bent in one smooth motion, grabbed his opponent's leg, and dragged it up sharply. The thing tipped over with a yell, the Jotun inside the tank struggling to right itself.

Laughter was his only answer.

What's a Wonder Mop? Gar asked. *And what's an infomercial? I haven't ever seen that word in the dictionary you gave me.*

That's because Bethany Anne had the good sense to ban them, Shinigami explained. *I only know about them because Eric sometimes likes to pretend to do them for his guns. "But wait! There's more! For just seven easy bullets—"*

Barnabas was laughing as he ripped off one of the Jotun's legs, then decided to finish the fight and punched down as hard as he could, sinking into the movement. The tank shattered and he pulled his knife out of its sheath and plunged it down, impaling the Jotun's body.

It was a singularly unpleasant sensation to stab a jellyfish, especially when you knew that jellyfish was sentient, but Barnabas had no time to dwell on it. Jeltor was being overwhelmed.

Barnabas surged up and over the remnants of his opponent's bodysuit and slammed the pink Jotun into the wall, narrowly missing a jet of flame from Jeltor's arm.

"Sorry!" Jeltor called.

"No...problem..." Barnabas found a mechanical hand clamped around his neck as the Jotun hauled itself upright and dragged him with it. "So tell me..." He kicked, hit nothing, and leveled a punch at the thing's armpit. "Why...pink?"

Behind them, there was a shout of satisfaction. Gar apparently won his battle.

The purple Jotun was formidable, but it couldn't fight three of them. Jeltor was there with a chainsaw, cutting off the arm that held Barnabas' throat, and Gar had a clear shot at its tank while it was distracted.

Barnabas staggered back, massaging his throat.

"What did you say?" Jeltor asked him.

"Why was it *pink*?"

"Oh. Some of us are, you know." Jeltor gave a full-body ripple that looked a bit like a shrug.

As one, the group turned toward the last Jotun. It had frozen. It knew its comrades were dead, and Barnabas felt the faintest stirring of pity. What would it be like, to be blind and helpless against the people who had killed your team?

They did not deserve his pity. He reminded himself of that.

I'm jamming signals coming into the ship, Shinigami reported. *Someone is trying to get it to do something—and it's not that Jotun you're looking at. I think they're trying to destroy it remotely.*

Can you keep blocking them? Barnabas put a hand out to stop Jeltor and Gar from advancing. If they needed to get off the ship...

For now. But deal with it quickly—or better yet, get him off the ship where I can better protect you three.

Good plan. Barnabas grabbed one of the Jotun's arms. "Come on, friend, let's have a chat." At his nod, Gar took the other arm, and they dragged the Jotun along with them despite its attempts to stop them.

It was Jeltor's exclamation that stopped them. Both Gar and Barnabas looked down to see the water in the tank foaming and the creature thrashing desperately, sticking to the wall as it tried to get out.

"Son of a—" Barnabas muttered.

It was already too late. The thing went limp a moment later and drifted amidst the foam as Barnabas let the biosuit drop to the ground with a thud. It was clear the Jotun was beyond the reach of any treatment they could summon, and Barnabas felt a stab of regret—not to mention anger. Over the years, he'd seen more than a few government agents choose death rather than capture, and it was always a damned waste. The governments they served were never worthy of that loyalty.

He sighed as he stared down at the biosuit, with the body floating limply in its tank. "Come on," he told the other two. "Let's get off this death trap and let Shinigami examine it."

And then, he added silently, *we'll try to figure out just which government should be mad as hell at the Jotuns.*

They had the ship, and Biset raged about that. The amount of technology they'd discover was unacceptable, and he could only hope they wouldn't put it to use before the committee's plan was in its final stages.

But at least they didn't have Norwun. Gods alone only knew what Norwun might have admitted to. Biset could only be glad that he'd thought to include a kill switch in all of the team's suits.

Although, perhaps...perhaps he should not have killed Norwun so quickly. Now, with Norwun dead and no interrogation, there was no easy way for Biset to learn more about the alien ship Barnabas had apparently encountered. Norwun might have turned the tables on him and learned some useful detail.

Biset thought about this, his tentacles lashing. There were too many unanswered questions here, and none of the potential answers boded well for him. He had watched the battle, and he still could not believe his eyes. It was beyond belief that the human and his crew had managed to kill as many as they had, ripping the biosuits limb from limb. The Jotuns had fought Brakalons, after all. The suits were made strong enough that such things shouldn't happen.

What was this human *thing* that was stalking him? And what was the thing that looked like a Luvendi? That species should have shattered its bones with every punch it threw. The recoil from its weapons should have nearly killed it. There was no way it should be alive.

The Jotun, though... Biset's eyes narrowed. He knew who *that* was: Captain Jeltor, proving once again that he was a traitor.

And if Jeltor had joined Barnabas at Gerris Station after Barnabas had learned of another government's black ops' involvement, that could mean only one thing: Barnabas knew about the committee, as did Jeltor.

And the committee must, therefore, eliminate them before they could tell anyone else.

Had they already told the Navy? If they had, there was only one thing to do. Biset pondered. No, he decided. They had not told anyone else yet. There would be a flurry of activity amongst the top brass if they knew of the committee. No, Barnabas and Jeltor were trying to find proof so that they could expose everything.

That would be how he would lure them in, Biset decided. He looked at the biosuit in the corner, outfitted with the very latest technology.

He would fight them himself when they came. He'd seen the way they could fight, and he would not make the same mistakes Norwun had.

CHAPTER NINETEEN

"The alloy that makes up the plating is *very* interesting," Shinigami reported. "We were researching something similar but couldn't get it to work. Hopefully, they'll have some idea what to do with it in the labs. I couldn't tell what had been done to it."

She considered the stone chess board and slid a pawn forward.

Barnabas took a moment before answering to study the board. "What about the engines?" He didn't choose a move yet.

"Not much of note there." Shinigami sat back in her chair, mimicking his pose. It was surprisingly eerie, giving that she pulled it off down to the minutest detail. Barnabas sat up hastily. "You don't want to put a huge engine in a ship that can't handle it, so it's more the fact that the ship could handle it—and the crew," she added. "The speed at which that thing could take turns could *easily* knock all your artificial gravity out and burst you open on a wall."

"How...vivid."

She flashed him a smile, ignoring his dry tone. "I think the reason they could take it was something to do with their tanks. I scanned Fizzy McSudsalot but didn't see anything special. Why are you laughing?"

"That foam killed him," Barnabas explained. He had his head in one hand, and his shoulders were shaking with laughter. "Oh, I'm a bad, bad man for laughing at that."

"You beat one half to death with its own arm. You were already not the purest angel there was."

Barnabas sighed. "I knew *that* much, yes. I think that honor goes to one of the puppies—though they're not puppies anymore, are they?"

"Not even a little bit. All big, shaggy death-monsters. Cuddly death-monsters." Shinigami shrugged. "They were probably pretty pure once, though."

"The world corrupts," Barnabas said philosophically. He moved one of his knights and took a sip of coffee—the thick, tar-black mix he'd learned to enjoy in Italy.

"Anyway, there *is* a lot they'll like, and I've left it for them to come get. They know about the attempted remote destruct, so they'll be careful with it."

"Good, good." Barnabas watched her choosing her move. Shinigami had gotten better at using her body's eyes to look at things. She even leaned a little closer to the board when she looked at it.

When she looked up, her face was grave. "It wasn't suicide. The first one was—the ship that intercepted us near the *Srisa*. This one wasn't."

Barnabas grasped her meaning. "He would have played ball with us, then."

"And so they had to kill him," Shinigami agreed. "Which

they didn't do before, which means they were almost certainly watching the fight. They know I can block their signals—at least, I could when those signals went to the ship because it was plugged into the station—and they know how you fight."

Barnabas, however, had thought of something else. "They know Jeltor is involved."

"Yes." Shinigami's eyes strayed to the door as if she were worried he might be listening. "He was wise to bring his family."

Barnabas sighed. He leaned his elbows on his knees and rubbed his temples as he thought. "And he just thought this was about the Yennai mutiny," he said quietly. "I got him involved. I didn't have to."

"That's just stupid," Shinigami snapped with her usual tact. "It was a Jotun Naval captain who died. Why would you *not* ask the one you knew for information about him? There would be no reason to hold back from doing that."

Barnabas nodded contemplatively. "I suppose you're right." His eyes tracked her as she moved a bishop into the space vacated by her pawn, and he frowned. "It was your pawn on the *other* side that was out before. I remember because I chose my side for the knight."

"Damn," Shinigami muttered. She switched the pieces around.

"I had a serious moment where I regretted the mortal danger a friend was in, and you were cheating at chess."

"To be fair," Shinigami said, holding up a finger, "*you* suggested we play a game of chess, and I think we both knew what that meant."

Barnabas grinned at her. Their games had abounded

with cheating since they first began playing chess together, and it had been the subject of several good-natured "fights." Gar still refused to be in the room with them while they played.

"In any case..." Barnabas moved his knight toward the center and forward. "It's beginning to seem as if we all underestimated the lengths the Jotun Senate would go to—which, I have to say, I would not have seen coming. My opinion of them was extraordinarily low."

"You and me both." Shinigami's eyes were wide as she shook her head. "What are they doing that's worse than selling out their *own* people to someone like Koel Yennai?"

"Something that involves another government," Barnabas said softly. "Apparently." He looked up at her. "And what would that be, do you think? What would Huword have been involved in that touched another government like that?"

Shinigami curled one leg under her and pulled the other knee up under her chin as she thought. The movement reminded Barnabas of Tabitha's more contemplative side—assuredly, not a side of her anyone saw often.

"What do we know?" Shinigami asked quietly. She wasn't looking at Barnabas, or at anything. "Huword pretended to be everyone's friend to get information about them."

"It may not have started that way," Barnabas said. "Some people seem to attract confidences. Over time, that familiarity breeds contempt."

"Why?"

"Honest question?"

"Honest question." Shinigami shrugged. "I hear a lot of confidences."

"Ah, I suppose you would as an AI." Barnabas considered. "I think it may be that over time, the secrets take a toll. One learns terrible things and starts to believe that everyone they meet is venal, self-absorbed, cruel..." He shrugged. "I saw it often with the other monks and priests. Some had come to believe that there was nothing worth saving in humanity."

"And you?" Shinigami asked curiously.

"I never inspired many confidences." Barnabas seemed amused. "I was in the monastery, for one thing, but I was also still struggling to keep myself sane. I hardly seemed like the sort of person who would welcome confessions."

"Hmm." Shinigami considered this. "Wait. You don't seem worried that I might have heard some of *your* confidences."

"I don't have any secrets," Barnabas said, amusement growing. "I can't think of anything that's happened since we started working together that would I would want to be secretive about."

"You need to live a little."

"We're getting off-topic," he told her, although he was still smiling. "And that was due to baseless speculation on my part about Huword. We don't know how it started, but we know that at the end he was feeding secrets to the Jotun Senate."

"And doing something else." Shinigami swayed from side to side contemplatively as she thought. "What if it has to do with his demotion? Someone found out about what he was doing and demoted him."

"Why would they also bother killing him?" Barnabas asked quizzically.

"One of two reasons." Shinigami held up two fingers at once. "First, because they thought demoting him would be enough of a punishment, then they realized they wanted to hurt him more. Second, because they wanted to get him out to the middle of nowhere to kill him."

Barnabas shook his head, frustrated. Neither of those rang true for him. "What I don't get is why they're so secretive. Jeltor is right; he should have been told. Whoever in the Navy figured out what Huword was up to you'd think they would have told the others. And this assassination seemed to be carefully planned. It wasn't a spur-of-the-moment thing, right?"

"I don't know. By the way, are we just giving up on chess?"

"I think so." Barnabas looked at the board. "I can't focus."

"I like that—easy win."

"Opportunist." He gave her a look. "All right, let's try to state the facts a different way. A Jotun assassin sent by the Navy killed Huword, but the people who are now chasing her, and us—the black ops group under Jotun senatorial control—seem worried that another *government* might be in play. What do we make of that discrepancy?"

"I don't *know.*" Shinigami groaned and flopped her head down theatrically. "Hey, maybe it was a bunch of things at once. Everything caught up with him at the same time."

"That is depressingly likely," Barnabas said. "He sounds like a nasty piece of work." He considered. "You know what? I think we need to go talk to Ferqar again."

"The assassin is still on the station, you know."

"I don't think we're going to get anything out of her," Barnabas replied. "It sounds like she made up her mind not to tell us anything, and short of torture, which we *won't* be using, I can't think how we'd persuade her. Ferqar, though…there were some cracks in his armor."

"I'll send another message to Kelnamon—and one to Ferqar as well. I've found some of the channels the Jotun Navy uses. Do you think the *Srisa's* moved?"

Barnabas felt a sudden chill. "If they haven't, they should have. We should have told them to move as soon as we realized the Jotun government was involved and things didn't add up. What direction did this Jotun ship come from?"

"I can't tell," Shinigami said honestly. "Their programming is like them—all blobby and incomprehensible. I could only block the signals because I could understand the *station's* computers."

It was Barnabas' turn to groan. "All right, send a message to Captain Kelnamon in pretty much every direction you can think of, and then one for Ferqar. In both, pass on what we need from the other one."

"You think they're working together?" Shinigami asked, surprised.

"I'm not certain. Actually—no, I'd bet they're not working together. Kelnamon struck me as fundamentally honest, and not as if he was holding something back. But I think one of them might persuade the other to talk to us if they're hesitant."

"I'll send the messages," Shinigami said. "Jeltor may also have an idea of how to get hold of Ferqar. For all I know, the channels I found are the sort everyone's supposed to use and don't."

"I'm hesitant to involve Jeltor any further than he already is." Barnabas felt a stab of worry.

Shinigami snorted. "He's in it now, and it's a good bet that they know as much. There's nothing to be gained from him sitting the rest of it out."

"We give him a choice," Barnabas suggested gravely.

"He'll help," Shinigami predicted. "He's *pissed* about this guy. If there's dirt—and, let's be honest, there's clearly tons—he wants it to come out."

"We give him a choice," Barnabas repeated.

"*Fine.*" Shinigami rolled her eyes. "Those messages have been sent, by the way, by every means I know of to send them. What now?"

"Now I go talk to Jeltor, and you get Gar and Tafa to the conference room. We'll see if either of them can make heads or tails of this." Barnabas ran a hand through his ginger hair. He'd taken to changing his appearance every so often, usually regarding his hair color and cut, and he was enjoying the reddish brown—although Shinigami liked to tease him about it.

He sighed.

"What is it?" Shinigami was replacing the chess pieces. Barnabas caught a flicker out of the corner of his eye and realized that she'd replaced one of the pieces with a hologram. What her aim had been, he wasn't entirely sure—but he opted not to mention it in the hopes that he'd get to see her plan unfold soon.

In response to her question, he only shrugged. "I wish we could even think of a theory that fits, but *nothing* fits the facts we have, and every new thing we learn only seems to make things less clear."

Shinigami considered.

"Well, *someone* killed him," she said finally. "And they had a reason. So it's not like it's senseless; it just seems that way."

Barnabas nodded, somewhat heartened by this. "That's true. I'll see you in the conference room."

CHAPTER TWENTY

It took two hours of dedicated work before Kantar could be sure that she was safe to contact her employers.

She knew about the Senate's lackeys, of course. She had watched every piece of the pantomime unfold, knowing that they were coming after Barnabas because of her—but knowing, too, as she listened in on the conversation, that she could not be of any help to him. Any aid she gave might trace back to her, and they *could not* find her.

Because they did not know why she had been hired, or who she was. And, of all things, she watched Barnabas hit upon the one suggestion that would frighten them the most: that another government had found out about what they were doing.

How could he have known? She could only wonder at first, awestruck that he had put together the pieces.

Then she realized the truth: he *didn't* know. He had just been looking for a way to keep them talking while his AI broke through their control of the station. She knew about

Barnabas. She'd done her research after he helped the Navy stand against the Yennai Corporation. His AI was said to be one of the most advanced in known space.

The Etheric Empire had been far ahead of its time in many ways. Kantar knew that the Jotuns had been looking into many of the technologies the Empire—and now the Federation—had at its disposal.

Whoever he worked for now, Barnabas had a good team. He was resourceful and honorable. Kantar wanted to trust him with the rest of the plan.

It wasn't her choice, though. Her employers were the ones who needed to approve this. Therefore, she took the risk of contact. Even with the Senate's lackeys dead and their ship under Barnabas' control, she took every precaution.

The call spent long enough connecting that she knew they were questioning whether they should answer. When they finally did, it was from a nondescript white room that could be anywhere.

"What has gone wrong?" Gil asked her at once. She did not know his full name. His suit was optimized for scientific research and surveillance, but she knew no more than that.

"Nothing is wrong," Kantar said. "The Senate sent a team, but not for me."

"What?" That was Wev, who was much like Gil, except that Gil was always quiet and Wev was always in motion. His tentacles churned through the water of his tank in a constant swirl. "Who would they have gone for?"

"You're at Gerris Station," Gil said. It was a question of a sort.

"Yes." Kantar nodded. "Brakalon law says that a ship must be brought to a halt after a murder. We drifted for a week before someone came—Ranger One, formerly of the Etheric Empire."

Both stilled. Not everyone would be aware of who Barnabas was, but Jotun Intelligence knew. It was their databases she had gone into when she was researching him. Neither Gil nor Wev spoke after she said that. They were watching her warily.

"Word of Huword's death was sent to the Senate," Kantar explained. "Other ships that had tried to approach the *Srisa* had been destroyed by one of their watchdogs. They wanted their ship to get there first to investigate. When Barnabas' ship docked, I thought they bought him."

"They had not?" Gil sounded suspicious.

"No." Kantar rippled to show amusement. "I distrusted him and tried to subdue him. It was a miscalculation. He nearly caught me, and after I fled the ship, he pursued me here." She would explain all of that later. "The Senate's team found him here. They must have spoken to the crew of the *Srisa*."

Neither of her employers said anything, and Kantar sighed. This was the frustrating part about working with Intelligence. They rarely offered *anything* to make a conversation go well. They just listened and watched.

"He would make a good ally," she said, laying her cards on the table.

Both responded to that. Shock showed in Wev's constant movements, and even Gil shot sideways in his tank.

"No," Gil snapped, recovering first. "Absolutely not."

"I agree." Wev backed up his partner without hesitation. "It's too dangerous."

"What's too dangerous is waiting," Kantar argued. "There's more to do."

"And we are doing it," Gil snarled. "We hired you for one thing, and you have done it. We are grateful for your aid. You will be paid."

"I don't care about the payment," Kantar argued. It was a lie. She did care; she had bills the same as everyone, and she had to lay low for a while in case the Senate found out about her, too. "I *care* about this. I'm useful, I'm a good asset, and they're so focused on Barnabas that I could still be helping."

"If they remain focused on Barnabas," Wev replied smoothly, "then he is *not* a good ally."

Kantar always forgot this about Wev. He looked nervous and usually waited for Gil to speak first, but every so often he would make a sly, sideways observation that shook her—and she wasn't even being interrogated. She shuddered to think what it would be like to speak to them if they were not on her side.

Gil was watching her, meanwhile. He did not say anything.

"Yes, they know of him," Kantar said, "but they will track him down now, no matter what he does. We might as well put that confrontation to good purpose. He could help us, and he *would*." She took a deep breath. "By accident, he guessed that another government might be involved. It was a shot in the dark; he was trying to scare them. But that's what they think is going on. That's who they think killed Huword."

The other two swiveled in their tanks and simply looked at one another for so long that Kantar guessed they must have some subvocal way of speaking to each other. That would be useful in Intelligence operatives, she guessed.

When they swiveled back they looked eerily similar, even moving the same way.

"Tell us everything," Gil said.

"Everything," Wev agreed.

Kantar did. She told them about the conversation they had seen and the conversation she'd had with Barnabas. They did not like that, she could tell, even though she had not told him much of anything.

"That was how he guessed," Wev said when she was done. "Because you let something slip."

"I didn't let anything slip," Kantar said angrily. "I told him deliberately. Maybe you don't agree with it—"

"We don't," Gil replied unequivocally.

"He could be a good ally! How many more do we need to take out before this is all over? We can't do it all on our own."

"We will take care of it," Gil said at last. "Not you. Certainly not him."

Kantar settled into mutinous silence.

"I think we should remind her," Wev said. He switched the video feed to his suit's sensory intake, and Kantar found herself jarred by the sudden change in perspective.

Wev got up and left the room, and she had a glimpse down a long hallway lined with doors. Wev chose one and opened it and went inside, with Gil behind him. As soon as they entered, Kantar knew why he had chosen this one.

The patients inside were kept behind panes of thick plastic. She could tell it was unbreakable because it was clear that the aliens inside had tried to break it. As Wev and Gil entered, they all showed their hatred with broken cries and hisses.

And their injuries… Kantar could hardly bear to look at them. Marks were healing all over their bodies, along with numerous scars.

"We've tried to rehabilitate them," Wev explained to her. His voice echoed strangely in her head, given her perspective. "We dare not let them out of the building, of course. The committee can't know that their experiments have been stopped."

"We couldn't let them out of the building even if the committee were finished," Gil continued. He was all business. Usually, they both were, but right now Kantar could hear genuine sadness. "We tried it with one of them, an Ubuara, and it nearly killed Wev."

Wev's biosuit gave a little shudder at the memory.

"An *Ubuara?*" She could not believe that.

"Have you ever seen a creature fight when it believes that is its only chance of survival?" Wev asked. "Have you seen a creature fight when it hates its opponent with all of its being and wants nothing more than to make it suffer? For that Ubuara, it was both. We killed it. It was not our intent, but it was the only way to stop it from killing *us.*"

Kantar found herself weeping. The mechanics were slightly different for a Jotun than for other species, but she still seeped salt into the water around her and tasted it on the tips of her tentacles. She could tell from their voices that they had not wanted to kill the Ubuara.

"The rest...we cannot chance it." Gil had recovered some of his composure, though not all of it. "We have given them food and made them as comfortable as we can, but they do not hate us any less. They have been driven mad." There was a pause, and then his voice changed. "Sometimes by accident we do the things that must have been commands of some sort. They obey, even though they hate us with everything they are."

Kantar was shaking in her tank. She did not want to see this.

And yet, she must. This was why she was here. This was part of what Huword had helped the committee do—and he had been prepared to do much more.

"We went through their notes," Gil continued. "Every one of them should be killed, but there is too much more to learn."

Horror and frustration surged within her. "Then why don't you let Barnabas help? He would help—he *would*! You've seen the things he's done, so you know he's honorable."

"It's that very honor that we can't trust," Gil snapped. After a pause, Wev turned his body so that Gil was looking directly into the sensors—at Kantar, all those millions of kilometers away. "That honor is what makes him dangerous to all of us. What would the Ubuara do to us if they knew about this? What would the Luvendi do? What would the *Brakalons* do?"

Kantar had no answer for that.

"We have to fix this ourselves," Gil said. "Their lives will be avenged—all who suffered for this. It may not be repaid in full measure, but those who are responsible *will* pay."

"But we cannot let any other species know of this," Wev agreed.

"We cannot." Gil picked up the thread; it was as if they were one person. "If anyone else knows, the Jotun people will suffer. There will be war. There will be..."

Kantar, seeing this in the flesh rather than simply in words on a screen, could only agree.

If anyone else knew of this, they would come down on the Jotuns with everything they had. She regretted ever speaking to Barnabas.

She could only hope that he would forget about all this and fight some other battle.

Barnabas was in his quarters reading a book of Luvendi poetry when the sensors beeped and the door slid open.

Shinigami gave a curious look at the book. "Luvendi... poetry? I thought they didn't do that stuff."

"They claim that they don't," Barnabas said. "But someone did. This stuff isn't bad." It was exceeding his expectations, but on the other hand, his expectations had been very low. The Luvendi did not have music, nor did they dance or tell many stories.

Whoever this renegade Luvendi poet was, they'd had to break every social convention they knew. That was impressive, if nothing else.

"What is it?" he asked Shinigami.

"We've received two messages," she said. "One from a Jotun admiral. I'm not sure which one, but if we trace it back, that appears to be the source. The message says there's information on Huword."

"The person who hired the assassin," Barnabas said slowly.

"So it would seem." Shinigami shrugged. "The other is from Ferqar. He's willing to meet."

"Is he?" Barnabas considered. "Ferqar first," he decided. "It's the same information, either way—or so I expect. Get the admiral to send more details if you can."

"I shouldn't tell them we'll be speaking to Ferqar?"

"In this case," Barnabas said, "I'm beginning to think we shouldn't tell anyone anything. The Navy has turned on itself, the Senate is sending black ops, and Lord only knows what other species have to do with any of it. No, don't tell the admiral anything yet. We'll see what Ferqar says and go from there."

CHAPTER TWENTY-ONE

Without any other comment, Kelnamon sent rendezvous coordinates for a meeting between the *Shinigami* and the *Srisa*. He was there when the door opened, and when Barnabas and Shinigami stepped out of the airlock, his smile was genuine if a little weary.

"Welcome back to the *Srisa*, humans."

"Thank you, Captain Kelnamon." Barnabas ducked his head in a small bow. "I must say, I was quite glad to hear that you had left your position in space."

"Broken our laws, you mean?" Kelnamon asked bluntly. "Yes, I did do that."

"With all due respect, Captain—"

"We could quibble over technicalities all day," Kelnamon interrupted. He fixed Barnabas with an uncomfortably shrewd glance. "I made my choice, and I would make it again—but Brakalon courts are not known for being accommodating." He shrugged his broad shoulders. "And you have more important things to worry about."

"Of course," Barnabas murmured. He followed

Kelnamon down the hallway in silence, but his mind was already forging ahead. He risked a glance at Shinigami. *Shinigami—*

Already on it. She gave him a small smile. *I assume you were going to say we should prepare a statement to the Brakalon justice system taking responsibility for the* Srisa *moving.*

Yes, thank you.

Should we send a muffin basket with it or something?

I think that would be overkill.

Barnabas was still smiling when he was shown into one of the few free rooms on the *Srisa*. A battered old table and chairs were the only furniture, and for decoration, there was what appeared to be a Brakalon motivational poster. A broad window looked out into space, however, making the effect much less claustrophobic than it might otherwise have been.

Ferqar was standing at the window, but he swiveled in his tank as Barnabas came in and gave a little bob that Barnabas thought might be a Jotun nod of greeting.

I think you can see their emotion in how *they ripple,* Shinigami said a moment later. *I want to collect a data set and then go to Jeltor to confirm some things.*

Good plan. Something tells me we're going to be interacting with more Jotuns before this is resolved, and I want to be able to tell when they're trying to hide their emotions. Although Barnabas could simply read the mind of any sentient being, he learned a lot from the interplay between the emotions they showed and what was going on in their mind.

He sat, and Shinigami took the seat beside him. Ferqar sat across the table, while Kelnamon let himself out of the room and closed the door behind him.

"So," Ferqar began, "what is this about? Not that I don't have my suspicions."

"Interesting turn of phrase," Barnabas commented. "I also have...well, guesses."

The mechanical head swiveled, and Ferqar bobbed in the water. "And what are your guesses?" Not much movement could be seen in either the jellyfish body or the tentacles. He was waiting, and his mind was surprisingly tranquil. There was no more fear—and no more guilt.

Barnabas took a moment to study him before answering, "I know you didn't kill Huword. I've spoken to the one who did. But it interests me that you had such an ironclad alibi, and it interests me, too, that you and Huword were out here where he wouldn't have access to backup."

Ferqar said nothing, although his mind went into overdrive. *Make sure you don't know anything,* a voice said in his memory. *Make sure you don't see anything.* Barnabas remembered the flavor of this memory, although the last time he'd felt it, it had been lost within the swirl of anger and fear in Ferqar's head. Then, Barnabas had not managed to catch the words.

He found himself getting angry now. "Oh, come now." He stared Ferqar down. "I am interested in *Justice*, not laws, and Huword deserved this. I have no intention of turning you over to the Jotun Senate—who, it has to be said, would not know Justice if it bit them."

Ferqar considered this. "I think I may have a mistranslation," he said finally. "What is a 'Justice' in your language? In our language, it is akin to retribution, and it cannot *bite*."

"It's a colloquialism," Barnabas said, realizing his mistake. "I simply meant, the Jotun Senate is so corrupt that they could not possibly enact any true Justice, and I doubt they have a use for the concept or even remember what it is."

"Ah. That's quite true." Ferqar sounded amused. He considered for a moment longer. "You want to know if I was part of the plot, then."

"Yes."

"May I ask why?" Ferqar sounded curious. "You say you know who did the act, and you must know, now, what he did. Why does it matter—"

"I don't know what he did," Barnabas explained. The fact that he was able to keep his voice level despite his rising anger was due to centuries of practice. Not only that, it was risky, laying his cards on the table like this. But he avoided half-truths when he could, and there had been far too many lies already. He was in no mood for them when he and Ferqar were on the same side.

This surprised Ferqar. He'd gone fluttering back against the edge of his tank, and the biosuit turned its head a few times as if he did not know what to direct it to do.

"I know Huword betrayed the Navy in the mutiny, and even before it," Barnabas said. "That much, I know. I thought that was why he'd been killed, but when I spoke to the assassin, I learned there was more to it, although she didn't—"

"Don't tell me who it was," Ferqar broke in quietly but with force. "I don't want to know. I don't want to know anything about how it happened. We agreed it was best if those among us did not know anything about each other."

Barnabas nodded. It was nothing to him either way, and it had probably been a wise precaution. It made sense of the memory he had seen, and the words Ferqar spoke now had the ring of truth to them—there was no deception in his thoughts. "In any case, the assassin told me that it was not her information to provide, but that Huword had done a lot more than I knew." He sighed. "And then, when interacting with the team the Senate sent—the team, I'm guessing, that Kelnamon moved the ship to avoid—I hit upon another truth: that other species, other governments, would be very angry about whatever it was Huword was doing. I don't know why, but I'm right, aren't I?"

Ferqar was quiet for a long time. When he spoke, he sounded broken.

"Even I don't know all of it," he admitted. "I am sorry. I wish I could tell you everything. I've tried to make sense of what I know, but from what I can see it is simply… Is there a word in your language for someone who enjoys causing pain?"

"A sadist," Barnabas said precisely.

"Then that's what he was," Ferqar said. "A sadist. That's all I can think."

Barnabas was beginning to understand the shape of this. "He hurt other species."

"Yes." Ferqar wasted no time prevaricating. "I learned of the things he had done after—I don't know where to start. I think…hmmm. Let me start with this: I didn't lie when I said that my posting was a demotion. It wasn't anything big, as such things go. There wasn't a scandal. I just never got along with Admiral—well, it doesn't matter which one. It was enough that every time I was up for a promotion or someone else was up for my job, I was the one who got moved. I fought it for years, but in the end, I got moved here, to this posting. And there's no coming back from this one. Other captains will live out their lives knowing that when we had to defend our people, they were there at the mutiny. They risked everything and fought our enemies. I was too far away. I'll never be able to say that. I'll never do the things I dreamed of. I'll be forgotten."

Barnabas could say nothing to this. The raw hurt in Ferqar's voice was almost too much to bear, and he could imagine all too well how it would have happened. It would have been little things here and there; never an overt abuse of power, simply repeated disregard for Ferqar's achievements over the years. *I don't know why I've just never liked him much*—Barnabas could easily imagine the conversations.

And so Ferqar had been passed over time and again, and the tiny cruelties had robbed him of what should have been his victory—a victory he shared with the rest of the Navy.

Shinigami said quietly, "I am sorry."

"It is done," Ferqar said. "It is over. I have to make my peace with it."

She nodded.

Ferqar stirred, then. "So what I told you about how two captains might talk when they were demoted—that was true. I would have done that for him...if things had been different."

"You already knew something about him," Barnabas guessed.

"I did," Ferqar confirmed. "I was talking with another scout once, one of the ones who control their craft, just them. It's...not a life for everyone. It gets lonely. But the ones who do it, they love it. He said he'd been out near the border with—" He broke off. "Is the captain listening?"

"No," Shinigami answered. "He left, and there aren't any listening devices in this room. He's the type who doesn't want to know intrigue."

"Thank you," Ferqar told her. "The scout said he'd seen a ship near the Brakalon border."

"Huword's ship," Barnabas guessed.

"Yes. And he shouldn't have been there—well, it wasn't his *mission* to be there. The scout didn't engage. Those ships fly cloaked, and he wasn't going to break that cloak by sending a message. The ship wasn't even *doing* anything, just flying slowly through a few systems. It could have been a classified mission. It could have been open knowledge, him hunting down someone who'd hurt him. It could have been nothing, but the scout said he followed them anyway because something felt off about it."

Barnabas waited, worry rising in his chest.

"There's a Brakalon colony in one of those systems," Ferqar said. "It was attacked not long after. I was the one who found it out, not the scout. I heard about it, and I decided to do some investigating on my own. There weren't any survivors at the colony, and it was made to look like Skaine had done it. Who would doubt that? But I know our weapons." The sensory plate turned in Barnabas' direction and stared at him unmoving. "I knew it was one of our ships, and I knew whose it had been."

"The Jotuns wanted the colony," Barnabas guessed.

"If they did, they haven't done anything with it. And they aren't all dead, the civilians. Some are *missing*."

Barnabas, who had been about to guess mining, closed his mouth.

"I looked up the rest of his missions," Ferqar continued. "He's had a lot, and his ship hasn't been where it was supposed to be very often. A lot of things like this. It took some doing, but I found other places where he'd done the same thing. I couldn't prove it, of course."

"He's taking captives?" Shinigami asked.

"So it would seem. A few on each colony, and he'd *done* things to them." Ferqar's revulsion went so deep he could barely form the words. "He is a sadist," he said again.

"And so another government might *well* have sent a black ops team to kill him," Barnabas mused. "But..."

"But it doesn't explain how the Senate is involved," Shinigami picked up. She looked at him.

"Exactly." Barnabas shook his head. He looked at Ferqar.

"When I was contacted by—I don't know who it was—I knew exactly how to get him onto this transport," Ferqar said. "I made sure he knew that there weren't any Naval sources on board to listen in on this. I told him that we had to stick together through these demotions, through all the tedium—through all the stupid border patrols past meaningless little alien colonies. I told him a little about my last few routes and mentioned remote alien colonies. All the details were made up, of course."

Barnabas shook his head slightly. Ferqar had, indeed, set the perfect trap. Huword must have thought he could pump the other captain for details on vulnerable remote alien colonies.

"*His* move wasn't a demotion, was it?" Ferqar asked.

"That was what I couldn't understand. I thought the admiralty board knew about it, and… I don't know what I thought. But it was the Senate who had him moved, wasn't it? They were *sending* him to kill these people. *Why?*"

"That, I don't know." Barnabas shook his head. "But you have to hide. You've seen far, far too much, and the people who came after us on Gerris Station were looking to tie up any loose ends."

"We'll hide," Ferqar said. "Kelnamon's no fool. He knows people are looking for the *Srisa* or anyone who was on it. We're going dark after this. He didn't even want to meet with you, but I wanted to know whose side you were on—and, if you were on ours, I wanted to know what you would do. Now…I hope you'll hurt whoever Huword was working for."

Barnabas gave a small smile. "I'll find out who they are," he promised. "And I will bring them to Justice. Thank you for your help."

He and Shinigami left with a brief goodbye to Kelnamon, and it was only when they were back on their ship that Barnabas said, with feeling, "What the *hell* was this guy up to?"

Even Shinigami looked lost. "I have no idea." She looked disturbed. "But it was *nothing* good."

CHAPTER TWENTY-TWO

"All right." Barnabas sat down in the conference room, adjusting the fit of his vest minutely before bringing up several systems and images. He looked at Jeltor's wife. "This will involve highly classified information regarding your government, which may be…distressing. If you'd like not to see it, I understand."

"Thank you, but I will stay." However Jotun biosuit voices were chosen, hers was a pleasing contralto. "When Jeltor was taken as a hostage, I thought it was the worst thing that could befall us. Then I learned he was walking willingly into more danger at your side, and I was even more afraid. And then the Senate condemned him for what he'd done, and I realized I had known nothing about my own government. Whatever they did, the least I can do is see it."

Barnabas nodded silently.

"And," she added wryly, "I'd at least like to *know* where he's running off to the next time he goes."

Jeltor gave a strangled, guilty-sounding noise.

"He gave me a big speech just before this," his wife explained, "telling me that he was only going to provide you with information, and definitely *not* go charging off. Given past experience, I have to assume that 'charging off' is exactly what he'll do."

Gar was trying to stifle his laughter, but Shinigami didn't even bother. She chortled as she sat back in her seat.

"She's got your number, Jeltor."

"Yes, well." Jeltor made the same, embarrassed sound again. "I suppose we'd better get on with the planning, then."

Barnabas hid a smile. He might not have let the meeting stray into the weeds like this, but the truth was, he wasn't looking forward to going over this information again. Shinigami had found the incidents Ferqar'd mentioned and had passed the highly graphic information to him with no comment. Even she was disturbed, and she did not get disturbed easily.

Barnabas sighed now and nodded to the screen. "We still don't know who hired the assassin," he said. "I'll put that out there. For all I know at this point, it *was* a foreign government. Ferqar took precautions to make sure he wouldn't know who he was working with."

"Ferqar was in on it?" Jeltor asked interestedly.

"He...was the one who got Huword into position. He knew some of the things Huword had done and was somehow connected to whoever hired the assassin." Barnabas shrugged helplessly. "There are a lot of blanks, so here's what we do know—and, again, this will be disturbing, and I won't think less of any of you for not wanting to see it. Leave if you need to."

The rest of the room settled into anxious silence as he brought up the list of colonies. There were Ubuara, Brakalon, Yofu, Jotun, Torcellan, and even Skaine colonies.

"These colonies," Barnabas explained, "were attacked, and most of the inhabitants were taken elsewhere. Some of the civilians were killed in various painful ways—there are pictures, but take my word for it—and their bodies were left. The attacks were pinned on slavers and pirates, but we can be fairly certain that all of them were either perpetrated by Huword or somehow enabled by him."

Jeltor's wife made a surprised sound. Jeltor floated to the very edge of his tank, close to her, and she moved closer to him, as well. Although they could not touch, they seemed to take comfort in each other's presence.

"We don't know his purpose," Barnabas explained. "Ferqar suggested that it might be a personal thing on Huword's part, but I can't believe that to be true. Huword's ship had a crew aboard it, and surely someone would have spoken up if they were doing things like this. Moreover, the Navy did not react to the fact that Huword's ship was rarely where it was supposed to be or doing the things it was supposed to be doing."

"These are all border colonies," Jeltor said suddenly. "And Huword had just been demoted—we thought. It wasn't a demotion, was it? They were sending him to do this."

"So it would seem," Barnabas agreed. "Which begs the question of who else in the Navy was in on this, because it certainly seems that Huword was acting in the interests of the *Senate,* instead."

There was a long pause.

"Burn the whole thing down," Shinigami suggested finally, "and start over."

"At this point, that might be wise." Barnabas rubbed his forehead. "That was a joke," he told Jeltor.

Jeltor, however, was unamused. "Maybe it shouldn't be," he said grimly. "Maybe she's right."

There was silence after his words. He had fluttered away from the wall of his tank and was now on the other side of it, away from his wife's presence.

"Jeltor." She spoke quietly.

He said nothing.

"Jeltor, the Navy has many good captains."

"We thought *Huword* was a good captain!" he flared angrily. "And now there's another traitor. The Senate can't be trusted, we've been abducting people and torturing them, and gods only know what else—"

"Every species fights corruption." Barnabas cut him off. "Every one. On Earth, humans did horrible things to one another. They would say it was in the name of science or progress or any number of good things they warped to serve their purposes, and the process of fixing all of that was messy and difficult. But it can be done."

No one said anything for a while.

"We should focus on what we're going to do," Gar suggested. "By which I mean, where we're going to look for information. We don't know the whole story yet. You know what I learned, working as a bureaucrat? Bureaucracies are *big*. It is genuinely possible that no one in the Navy noticed what Huword was doing."

"Or that several of them noticed at the same time," Barnabas agreed, seeing a chance to bring them to his next point. "We've been contacted by one of the admirals. We don't know which, but Shinigami believes that's who it is after having traced them. They say they have information about Huword."

"It's worth noting," Shinigami pointed out, "that this could easily be fake."

"Which is why we need a plan," Barnabas said smoothly. "We stood against the Yennai fleet and took their headquarters with hundreds of mercenaries trying to stop us. We've already stopped one of the Senate's black ops teams. We can assume that if this is a trap, it will be a good one— given that they successfully got us to think it was an admiral."

"Yeah." Shinigami nodded. "If this mission had been going another way, I wouldn't even question it. The way this one is going, let me tell you, I *checked* to see if it was fake. I checked a *lot*. I found nothing. I'm still suspicious."

"That's wise." Gar sounded weary. "There is no group of people as vicious as leaders who have something to hide. They'll throw everything at you that they can and tell you that you can't come after them because it will bring the whole organization down." He was looking at Jeltor now. "They'll tell you that showing how rotten and corrupt the Senate is, or the Navy, will make you a traitor to your people. They'll say the best thing to do is quietly get rid of the people who did all those things and just let it be forgotten."

"And what is the best thing to do?" Jeltor asked brokenly.

Gar sighed. "I don't know. When this comes out, no matter if it was one rogue Naval captain or a whole Senate conspiracy, it's going to do a lot of damage. But if you *don't* expose it, how will people know how bad things were? *Something* enabled Huword to keep getting away with this. Some part of the system wasn't working. You have to fix that."

"And there's the matter of Justice," Barnabas added. "And truth. People deserve to know what happened to their families, and instead of things being done secretly and silently, they should be done openly. Pushing all this under the rug is a sign that things aren't being done judiciously."

"So are we going to talk to them?" Jeltor asked. "Whoever they are."

"Most certainly." Barnabas smiled. "Either they'll be helpful in one way—because they're on our side—or they'll be helpful in another because we'll know more about who's trying to hush this up. Now, let's do this in order. Shinigami, what are your guesses about what we'll be facing?"

Shinigami brought up a spread of ships, formations, and companies.

"Here are the known types of ships in the Jotun Navy, plus the specs I was able to pick up from the black ops ship *and* the ship that tried to attack us near the *Srisa.* I'd say our best bet is to arrive far ahead of schedule, coming in cloaked. We can send a rendezvous message and then tell certain buoys and stations we pass to send pings from us at slower intervals than we're going. If they're tracking us via station data, they'll think they have more time before we arrive, and we'll get there during their setup phase."

She looked very pleased with herself.

"Good plan," Barnabas said. "Now for stress-testing. Let's start with what happens in case of a physical ambush when we get off the ship, and then talk about what happens if they see through our cloaking..."

Biset's tank was inserted into his suit and he wiggled his body, connecting with the various sensors and chemicals in the water. From here, he could touch certain controls and manipulate others with chemical inputs.

The process of creating the tanks had been fraught, and many Jotun had died trapped.

Much like what had happened to Huword. Biset shuddered delicately. That had been quite a loss. Huword had been the perfect agent, well-liked by everyone and willing to engage in any project without asking questions.

He'd killed a few of the captives, of course, but that sort of thing was to be expected. In any case, there were always more. Every species had those who left their safe inner planets and ventured to distant colonies.

They knew the risks.

The attunement to the biosuit was complete, and Biset strode out into the hallways of his ship. They were close and confining, with no windows. Windows were structural weaknesses, and Biset was always logical about such things. He would view his assets from the bridge on a viewscreen.

The images were already there when he arrived and took his place at the big command table. His bridge crew stood at attention, bobbing in their tanks in greeting as he went past.

On the screens was the last remnant of the Yennai fleet. Confiscated after their surrender, it had been locked away at once by the Navy, who claimed that their need to examine it was above that of the Senate.

But the Senate had Huword—or, at least, Biset's committee did. They hadn't asked him to steal it, only to provide its location and a way around the security measures. Biset had known that the time might come when he would need a fleet.

Now he was just glad that he had asked before Huword was killed.

His eyes narrowed as he stared at the fleet. It was impressive, yes, but even when Barnabas was dead, Biset would still not know which alien government had found out about the committee and killed Huword.

They were going to have to accelerate their schedule, and he did not like that—especially since the reports coming out of the facilities had changed lately. Once, they had been full of detail, and the scientists had enjoyed their work. Now the reports were flat and very basic. It was as if the workers there had entirely lost interest, even though they continued to hit their targets.

Biset would need to investigate that as soon as he was done with Barnabas. He turned his head to look at a nearby officer. "Where is the *Shinigami* now?"

"Several hours out, sir." The officer spoke crisply. "We caught a ping from Gerris Station."

"I thought he was at Gerris Station."

"He left briefly, sir."

"Find out where he went," Biset ordered. "And find me the *Srisa*. I asked for its location two days ago."

"Yes, sir." The officer looked worried, but he knew better than to complain of an impossible task. Those in Biset's service succeeded...or were killed.

CHAPTER TWENTY-THREE

The *Shinigami* arrived four hours ahead of schedule, hurtling toward the out-of-the-way Jotun colony that had been specified by their contact. Even though it had several factories and a resort no one had bothered to name it, so it was still known by its star system and planetary number.

Barnabas had been on the bridge for a good hour before they arrived, pacing back and forth.

He had insisted on leaving Jeltor's wife and children at a location that had functioned as a safe house of sorts for Rangers—back when this sector was the middle of nowhere, of course, but still territory they owned and protected.

He had wanted to leave Tafa as well, but she refused to go. "It's my home," she'd told him, almost offended. "You're my friends. I'm not going to sit somewhere else twiddling my thumbs. Someone needs to fly the ship if you and Shinigami both go off to fight."

Shinigami had only a limited processor in her body,

and communicated Etherically with the ship, doing her "thinking" on board and simply sending the answers to the body, but Barnabas didn't tell Tafa that. She was determined to stay and help, and he respected her more for not running from danger.

She got to the bridge closer to their arrival time, as did Shinigami and Gar. The two of them had been practicing sparring together, and the Jotun assassin still inspired Shinigami. She was already moving more smoothly and seemed more at home in her body, while Gar seemed to be learning more by being a teacher than a student.

Jeltor, who had been speaking with his wife over holo, came onto the bridge as the first view of the planet came up on the screens.

And between them and it were several ships.

Several Yennai ships.

"Well, there's our answer," Shinigami stated.

"It could be that they know about the meeting and are trying to block us from going to it," Barnabas pointed out. He took a seat, his armor gleaming dully in the light. "Whatever the case, though, let's give the people on Gokrun III a show, shall we?"

"*Good* plan." Shinigami flipped her hair over her shoulder and crossed her legs. Under her control, the ship sped up slightly, and the missiles began to prime.

They were facing a standard destroyer formation, seven ships with three in a row in the middle, and two each on both the top and the bottom, making a hexagon. At any rate, that seemed to be the formation they were approaching, but they were still getting into position.

"Look there." Shinigami panned the viewscreen to show a tiny ship above the battle.

It was small, yes, but well-armed. Even though it did not have the same number of scars and scorch marks as the black ops ship—in fact, it was nearly pristine—it was clearly of the same make.

"How close can we get without them seeing us?" Barnabas asked Shinigami. "The person who's orchestrating all this is on that ship, I *know* it."

She nodded, agreeing with his assessment. "To be honest with you, I don't know how close we can get. We can try. The question is, what are you going to do if we manage it?"

"Interrogate him," Barnabas said promptly. "Them. Whoever they are. I suppose there might be more than one. The destroyers will have to come about, and they won't want to fire on us if we're close to that ship."

"You're making assumptions." She considered the ships as they glided closer, still unseen. "I wonder how they're flying those. They weren't made for Jotun captains."

"We *can* fly ships the normal way," Jeltor pointed out. "The biosuits let us do that."

They considered, and Shinigami looked at Barnabas. "Whoever this is, we're not going to get a better opportunity to take the last of the Yennai fleet by surprise. We have the chance to take down seven destroyers right now. I say we do it—and before you ask why we must, just consider. We *are* going to have to fight them at some point."

Barnabas' mouth twitched. "I suppose you have a point. All right, then, let's finish them off and hope our friend doesn't get away while we do so."

Shinigami gave a small, pleased smile.

"All right, these ships don't have a forward and a back, but like every other ship I've known, they *do* have a top and a bottom. We're going to take out the center bar of the formation first. They're still very loosely aligned so we can do it quickly. If we're lucky we'll be able to take out the top two as well, but I don't want to count on that."

The *Shinigami* was already accelerating under the very bottom of the formation. Barnabas, who had nodded in acknowledgment of Shinigami's plan, sat quietly with his fingertips lightly resting on the armrests of his chair. He could pretend to be relaxed, but, his whole body was tense.

He had not expected such a reaction. Normally, he was either angry when he faced an opponent, or he was coldly logical.

But the sight of this fleet brought back memories— memories of himself floating helplessly in space, and Shinigami trapped. Their helplessness had only been a ruse, a trap their enemies had fallen into headfirst, but for both, the memory was very real and very wrenching.

Shinigami must have noticed because he felt the brush of her mind against his—not words, but instead simply an expression of shared memory. When he glanced at her, for the first time, he felt he saw *her*, not just the amalgamation of Tabitha's features and Bethany Anne's. Her profile, the set of her jaw, and the slight press of her lips showed her determination.

When they started working together, they would never have trusted one another enough to pull off that mission. It had taken danger and victory alike to get them to that point, and Barnabas realized he was grateful for it.

He'd had love once and lost it. He'd had siblings, and lost them as well. He'd had more than one life, first as a human and then as one of the Nacht, and finally—for he did view joining Bethany Anne as a rebirth of sorts—his life as a Ranger.

Now he had this, a friendship he had never expected. He looked at Tafa and Gar, at Jeltor, at the ship itself, and felt a renewal of his purpose.

Tyrants and corrupt governments were *always* defeated. Always.

Shinigami brought the ship up around the "back" of the formation. Although the ships were made to go in either direction, their engines placed to vent out the top and bottom of the ship in a diagonal pattern, the crew would be focused on one set of viewscreens. Any visible flicker would not, God willing, be in their line of sight this way.

On the approach, Shinigami hesitated slightly. "Center?" she asked Barnabas. "Or edge-in?"

"Center," Barnabas decided. "That way, if they spin out of control, they have more of a chance to hit something no matter which way they go."

"When you're mean, you're *mean.*"

"People who abduct and torture civilians should not expect me to be nice to them." Barnabas was unperturbed.

Shinigami laughed and accelerated, pressing all of them back against their seats. She saw Barnabas' look, "All right, I know I *could* calibrate the gravitics so that wouldn't happen, but it's much more fun when you can *feel* how fast the ship's going, isn't it?"

"Yes." Barnabas gave a small smile. "It is."

Shinigami waited until they were close. Three

weapons were primed, and Barnabas saw that she was aiming for the engine vents. Normally in a battle, these would be protected, but the shielding was not in place yet, and the normal swarm of fighters had not yet deployed.

If she nailed these shots, she'd take three ships down in quick succession.

To Barnabas' surprise, she paused for a moment and bowed her head before pressing the button. It seemed that she had become at home enough in her body to take pleasure in making a physical gesture to accompany her choice.

Were you...praying? he asked her.

To his surprise, she did not answer at once. *I don't know,* she said finally. *I was thinking about what I would do. Is that praying?*

He looked at her. *If you want it to be.*

This was not the time for an in-depth discussion, but that was enough of an answer for her for now. She turned back to watch the missiles with a wry smile. *Previously, I didn't consider what would happen after I fired my missiles. Now I do. I think it's your bad influence.*

He could hear the teasing, but the serious sentiment behind it gladdened him. He had come into their partnership afraid of his own anger, and afraid to enact his own Justice. Shinigami had given him resolve. He, in turn, seemed to have given her a sense of the gravity of taking a life.

Both were necessary for true Justice.

The *Shinigami's* cloaking now worked against Jotun ships, but even their algorithms were not enough to keep the missiles from being seen at the end. A storm of activity broke out; Shinigami's scanners showed a burst of communications and the engines flared—

It was not enough. Two of the missiles hit dead on and, as the crew of the *Shinigami* held their breath, the chain reactions devoured the Yennai destroyers from the inside out. The engines blazed out of control, and the ships swung out of formation.

She had damaged the third, the engine ports a gaping hole, but the missile had not gone into the engines themselves.

"They're crippled," Barnabas told Shinigami. "Go for the other four first."

Her quick nod told him that she'd made the same assessment. She dropped a scatter of missiles on the bottom two ships to make them wary of firing up at her and brought the *Shinigami* up in a smooth arc to shoot at the upper two.

An animal's belly was vulnerable, an area they would always protect instinctively, and sentient beings tended to do the same with the bellies of their ships. The two destroyers above them swung out of formation in a panic, each trying to angle itself down to meet the *Shinigami* head-on.

She was faster than they were. Even as they pointed their noses at her, she was sliding under them, keeping them off-balance so that they must turn and orient themselves again.

Barnabas did not see what she was doing until she did so again, and he laughed. She had successfully maneuvered them so that the two upper destroyers were now between the *Shinigami* and the two lower destroyers.

Jeltor was laughing as well, having seen her strategy before Barnabas did. "I'd have done the same," he called to her, "if I'd thought of it. I might not have."

Shinigami gave him a grin in response.

This time, as the missiles finished priming, she sent a dense cloud of fire at the two sets of ships. Any that got past the two upper destroyers would, after all, have a chance of hitting the bottom two.

Barnabas turned his head to look for the ship that had hovered above the plain of battle. As far as he could tell, it was gone.

"It's landing on the surface," Shinigami told him. She had seen him look. She paused as her fingers danced over the controls and three missiles shot from the belly of the ship. "I marked its trajectory, and we'll be paying them a visit when this is done."

Barnabas nodded. He had wondered if that mysterious ship would help them—and if it were an ally, it would have. There would have been communication of some sort, perhaps, or material aid.

But nothing had come from it.

This had only ever been a trap.

Cleaning up the last of the destroyers didn't take long. The Jotuns *could* fly ships without their tank interfaces, but they weren't very good at it...and these weren't the Naval captains, but operatives brought here by the Senate. They couldn't match Shinigami for speed when it came to reactions, and they couldn't enact their commands quickly enough in the unfamiliar ships.

The last ship tried gamely to bring them down, but even as it fired its full spread of missiles, the drifting wreckage of the other six ships got in its way. Its companion ship clipped it as it spun out of control and the missiles went wild. Between the debris and the *Shinigami's* countermeasures, the battle was over almost before it began.

Barnabas sighed. He did not like fighting those who had no real chance for victory.

But they had chosen their path—and he had a new target now. On the surface of Gokrun III was the mysterious person who had orchestrated all this.

He was looking forward to meeting them.

CHAPTER TWENTY-FOUR

Biset was in a fury as he strode out of his ship and into the underground bunker. Around him, robotic soldiers stirred to life, arming their weapons as they responded to his rage. He calmed himself. He could not hope to win this battle if he allowed his emotions to run away with him.

He should have known that Barnabas would triumph against the remains of the Yennai fleet. It had been a foolish mistake on Biset's part, but no other ship he'd seen could take on seven and survive.

And the last two times they had faced the Yennai ships had not been true encounters. Once, the fleet had been ordered to let them through—Ilia Yennai's ill-fated idea that letting Barnabas be cornered in the flesh by mercenaries would be a better way to kill him than being fired on by an entire fleet.

She'd paid for that mistake with her life.

The other times Barnabas had faced the Yennai Corporation, it had been with the backup of the Jotun fleet. Biset had assumed, therefore, that the *Shinigami* on its own would not be able to triumph.

Clearly, he had been wrong. More critically, he had expected Barnabas to play by the rules. The pings they had caught from the space stations and buoys had been a ruse. Whether Barnabas knew this was a trap, or he was just habitually suspicious, he had known enough to arrive when he wasn't expected.

Biset tried to calm himself. Barnabas would have to get off the ship to fight him. The bunker was too far below ground to be reached with bombs, and even Barnabas' strike team couldn't get through this many robotic warriors.

Briefly, he thought of Ilia Yennai, and he was worried. But this was different. Robots did not feel fear. They did not mourn when their comrades were destroyed.

The others who had faced Barnabas had suffered from a lack of resolve, but Biset would not have the same problem. Biset would triumph.

He wondered idly if he would show the committee the *Shinigami* and laughed quietly to himself. He knew he would not do so. He was the one who had faced the danger, so he would be the one who kept the spoils of war. The *Shinigami* and its AI would be his for the taking after this.

If Koel Yennai had wanted it so much, after all, it had to be worth something. Biset expected it to be booby-trapped, of course, but he'd find a way around that. It was just an AI, and he had learned in his years that any mind could be turned with enough time and the right leverage.

No one was incorruptible.

Unseen in the rafters above, Kantar knelt to watch Biset walk through the ranks upon ranks of robotic soldiers.

Gokrun III was theoretically a resort planet for the Jotuns. No one else wanted it with its salty, storm-tossed seas, but the Jotuns liked the novelty of it—and the Jotun Senate, apparently, used the bunkers on its smallest continent to hide their experiments.

It was well-protected, which had meant that there was no way she could get a ship in here on her own. Any ship would be noticed and scanned. The satellites in low orbit were highly-attuned and well-armed.

So she had done the only thing she could and gotten herself aboard Biset's private ship. To escape detection, she'd had to power herself down and hope he did not take long enough in space for her to suffocate. Luckily, he had not. There had been a long time of the ship drifting aimlessly, and then—just before they began their descent—there had been some quick maneuvers that suggested a battle.

They had not fired their weapons, however. She did not know what had happened, and there was no one to ask. It did not especially matter anyway. Biset would soon be dead. After Huword, he was their next target. Biset had been Huword's direct contact, and was, as far as Kantar could tell, one of the most dangerous members of the committee.

She wondered about sending Barnabas word that Biset had been killed. On the one hand, if he knew about Biset and was hunting him, he might break off his pursuit when he knew Biset was dead.

On the other hand, he might just be more curious. Barnabas, she had come to believe, was motivated not by revenge or vice, but by the search for truth.

That made him dangerous. She knew that. Gil and Wev had been very clear that Barnabas could bring their government crashing down, and Kantar knew they were right. If the committee's work were made public, every other government would turn on them.

And yet...she found that she respected Barnabas' quest for the truth. The thought of burying all this, dealing with it quietly, gave her a twisty feeling in her gut. It didn't seem right, somehow.

The Jotun people all suffering for the actions of a few didn't seem right either, however. And if Barnabas insisted that they must, what would she do?

She would kill Biset, she decided. *Then* she would decide what to do.

She stood quietly and followed his path, walking silently on the rafters above him. Biset was training to lead a robotic army, much like an admiral would lead many ships in battle. She would have to figure out how best to deal with that, but she had always been good at waiting and biding her time.

CHAPTER TWENTY-FIVE

"Landing sequence activated," said Shinigami's voice over the loudspeakers, "complete in thirty seconds."

Barnabas bounced on the balls of his feet as he waited at the blast doors. He heard clanking a moment later, and Jeltor came around the corner with Shinigami. Gar trailed them, speaking quietly with Tafa as he did the last check of his weapons.

One of the first things Barnabas had trained him to do was to take care of his weapons, knowing them inside and out and not expecting technology to rescue him. It was impossible to understand all the specialized technology, of course, but clean, well-maintained weapons and armor were essential for survival.

At the door, all of them nodded to one another, and Tafa gave them all smiles.

"Be safe," she told them, and she disappeared down the hall. Barnabas could tell she was very determined not to look over her shoulder at them or watch as they left the ship. She was worried but trying to control it as best she could.

He could not blame her. What was waiting for them down there, he could not say.

But he knew one thing... He was deeply curious, and he was *very* much looking forward to bringing the ringleader to Justice. Shinigami had been correct when she'd said that whatever Huword had been up to, it was nothing good.

The *Shinigami* set down so gently that when the doors opened Barnabas was alarmed.

"Don't worry, silly." Shinigami's smile was teasing. "It's all okay. We're down, and the atmosphere is breathable. But don't tell me—back in your day, you had to get where you were going in a horse-drawn carriage, and you felt every bump. You didn't even *need* to land."

Barnabas was laughing silently. "No, no, in my day we rode dinosaurs."

"Now *that* is a mental image I can get behind. I'm going to have them clone you a dinosaur."

"Bad idea," Barnabas warned her as they walked into the underground bunker. "Didn't Tabitha show you *Jurassic Park*?"

"Where do you think I got the idea?"

"I think you took the wrong lessons from that movie." He crossed his arms and looked around. "So, we're...underground?"

"You're a great detective. No wonder the Empire flourished under your care." She strode out and looked around the bunker with him. "But yes. These doors were supposed to be closed to us—but I swear, a toddler must have written those algorithms."

Barnabas smiled slightly. From the pride in Shinigami's voice, it was clear that the algorithms had been significantly harder to break than she was suggesting. When they first came to this sector, it had contained technology different than any they had seen, and both had struggled to adapt. They had managed, though, as their enemies were presently finding out.

He followed slowly, examining this place with care. The ceiling in the bunker was low, and long pools of water ran down the center and sides of the room. Like the seawater outside, it smelled of salt and kelp.

The room was also empty.

"I don't like this," Barnabas murmured. "It just reeks of a trap."

As if in answer, one of the doors lit up and a Jotun voice —recognizable by its faint mechanical whine—said, "Thank you for coming. I knew it would be difficult to get past the Senate's blockade, but if anyone could do it, you could."

Jeltor's eyes had narrowed, and he shook his head. *I don't know this voice. It's none of the admirals.*

I'll play along, though, Barnabas said. He strolled forward. "Are you going to show yourself? I promise we're on your side. We want to bring Justice—the same thing you want." *It nearly made me sick to say that.*

That's the problem, Shinigami commented. *Honorable people have trouble lying even for a good cause, but it doesn't bother dishonorable people.*

"I'm afraid it's too risky," the voice said. "And that antechamber may be bugged. I cannot give you this information anywhere the Senate might hear of it. I'll light the way to a safe place."

Safe for us to get filled with bullets, Barnabas guessed.

Now, now, Shinigami scolded, *they might be planning to drown us instead.*

They'd probably find that fitting, Jeltor agreed. *They don't like other species, and most Jotuns are at least a little bit annoyed that we're the only ones who are amphibious. Luvendi don't count, I'm afraid,* he told Gar.

We swim, Gar pointed out, annoyed.

You don't have to be carried around in tanks. If the Jotuns had their way, you'd all be in air tanks and all stations would be filled with water.

Everyone quiet, Barnabas said as they walked forward slowly, *and let Shinigami concentrate on mapping this place. I think it's safe to say that we want to go anywhere but where they're telling us to go.*

Pretty much, Shinigami agreed. *But we'll have to move fast when we choose an alternate route. I'm not in their systems yet, and they can see us.*

The group emerged into a second chamber and was immediately faced with a group of robotic warriors, all of whom leveled the arms of their suits to show the barrels of guns.

"On the other hand," said Shinigami cheerfully, "maybe we don't need to spend time trying to find the trap after all."

Barnabas didn't pause to chime in, but he was laughing as he charged the group. He grabbed one warrior by the arm and dragged it around to face its fellow soldiers as they began firing. Many bullets landed, some ricocheting off the heavy plate armor of the robots, but others finding their targets: joints and weak points that hissed and sparked as the bullets struck.

Interestingly, not only did his robotic warrior stop firing, they *all* stopped firing—at the same time.

He's controlling them remotely! Barnabas called over the Etheric connection.

He didn't wait to see how they used that information but instead launched into action. He hopped onto the head of his robot to look around the room, then made his way to the far back corner using the shoulders and heads of the warriors as stepping stones.

They tried to follow him with their guns, but whoever was controlling them was not used to the pace of hand-to-hand fights, especially when an enhanced human was involved. Barnabas landed lightly without even a close call and whirled, drawing his Jean Dukes.

The guns went off with a roar and two of the robots staggered, one having turned to face him, the other still facing the other way and trying to pick its target. Barnabas fired again, aiming for the column below the sensory panel—the equivalent of the neck on a biological fighter.

With their connection to their sensors and their remote control disabled some of the robots shut down, but with others, Barnabas seemed to have fried some of the central controls, and the robots began to short out. Their bodies shook, limbs moving spasmodically. One collapsed, and another began firing straight at the floor. The bullets hit the reinforced concrete and bounced, sending projectiles in every direction.

"Hit the floor!" Barnabas yelled. He had time to worry

on the way down that this might be too colloquial, but the rest of the group seemed to understand him just fine.

There was a scream, and his head jerked up—only for him to start laughing. The scream was apparently Shinigami's battle cry.

And what a battle cry it was! What she lacked in precision, she more than made up for in sheer power. Her body was the first produced by Bobcat's team, but they hadn't been sloppy in their work, and they'd done thorough testing. Now that she knew how to use it, she had more raw power at her disposal than Barnabas might ever be able to summon.

It was enough to make him feel just the tiniest bit annoyed for a moment before he shook his head good-naturedly and joined the fight.

If she were stronger, he would have to become that much better in his form to match her. He could already tell that their sparring was going to get a *lot* more painful, and he found himself mentally repeating Bethany Anne's adage with a smile: Pain is an excellent teacher.

Shinigami, unaware of his thoughts, had taken a page out of his playbook from last time and was ripping the limbs off some robots and using them to beat the others into the ground and push them into the pools of water. They weren't made to swim, and they sank quickly below the surface.

On the off chance that their enemy was *in* those pools, Barnabas started doing the same thing. Now that the circuits were exposed they were sparking like crazy, and he could only hope that the Jotuns were electrocuted to the point that they could not concentrate—although from what he could see, they must have liquid sensors that cut the power to their suits as soon as they were submerged.

Gar, meanwhile, seemed to have appointed himself Jeltor's personal bodyguard, although Jeltor had put a thin sheet of nearly-transparent armor over the front of his tank and was taking well-aimed shots at the robots that were still standing.

Battle always seemed to Barnabas to take both infinite time and yet pass in the blink of an eye. For what seemed like an eternity, the world was full of bullets firing and ricocheting, metal screaming, Shinigami yelling, and the close-quarters combat of mechanical warriors against biological ones. And then, just as suddenly, it was over, and the remnants of the robots were twitching on the ground before them.

Then Barnabas noticed that the water level was rising.

The smart thing to do, of course, would be to leave the bunker. But that would mean leaving his quarry, too, and he was not about to do that.

"Wait here!" he yelled to the others, and he took off into the bunker at a dead sprint. The pounding of footsteps behind him told him that no one had listened. "I said, wait there! Or, actually, leave!"

"Oh, hell no!" Gar called, a strange colloquialism coming from a Luvendi's mouth. "We're not going to let you have all the— Holy shitballs!"

Floodlights went on in the next chamber, where easily three times the number of robotic warriors faced them. The person controlling them must have learned their lesson because these did not wait. In unison, they raised their arms—and fired.

CHAPTER TWENTY-SIX

This time, Barnabas didn't have to yell anything. He heard the others throw themselves down, and the next moment an exceedingly strong hand grabbed him by the ankle and dragged him back through the doorway.

"Ow! Bones!"

"Sorry," Shinigami said unrepentantly, hauling him upright like a rag doll. "I figured your ankle would heal fine as long as you were, you know, *still alive.*"

"Yes." Barnabas hopped on the other foot while the bones knit themselves back together. "Thank you. I take your point."

Bullets were still whizzing through the doorway in large numbers, and the water was now up to their ankles and pouring into the room beyond.

"Does anyone have a plan?" Gar asked pragmatically.

Shinigami ducked into the doorway for a moment and then came back. There was an impact point where something had gotten her in the head, but she didn't seem to have noticed.

"I think the person controlling it all is at the back of that room," she said. "I guess those robots aren't going to run out of bullets for a while. He's going to try to drive us out of here with water and kill us with traps whether we do or don't fight."

"Well, then," Barnabas said, "looks like he's only given us one option, hasn't he? Try to kill *him* to stop all of this."

The rest of them nodded.

"Any particular ideas on that front?" Shinigami asked Barnabas. "I'm not quite as squishy as you are, but I don't think I can take *that* many bullets."

Barnabas considered. "Jeltor, tell me what you can about those things…and be quick about it since this water is rising fast."

Kantar lowered herself from the rafters carefully and began to work her way down the back wall.

She had feared the robots at first, but Biset was a fool. He was too afraid to let them function as they had been intended to, so he had put them entirely on manual control. He didn't trust them to utilize their auto-targeting or fire their guns only as the algorithms suggested.

It was the sign, in her opinion, of a weak leader. Biset only wanted to trust those things he understood instead of trusting that his orders had been carried out.

And he did not have the capacity, as the Jotun admirals had, to control that many different bodies, each with different objectives, all at once. There was a reason there were only two or three admirals per generation. It was a rare individual who could manage all of that without going mad.

So much the better, as far as she was concerned. With the robots taken off auto-targeting and Biset wholly concerned with Barnabas' strike team, Kantar had a clear shot at Biset. If Huword had deserved to die, Biset deserved something far, far worse.

She only regretted that she couldn't think of a worse death to give him, but when it came to things like this, it was better to take the shot and kill him, thus making sure he could never hurt anyone else, than to try to draw out his pain and take the chance of him surviving.

Much better.

She watched as the water began to rise, and then, as Barnabas and his team charged out of the doorway toward the robots, a thought came to her.

She didn't have to kill Biset. Not yet.

If she didn't, after all, between the water and the bullets, he would likely kill Barnabas and the entire strike team. And if he didn't, Barnabas would kill Biset—and then be weak and undefended against Kantar.

In one stroke, she could rid the Jotun of two enemies: one who sickened them from within, and another whose quest for Justice might hurt the innocent.

Kantar stopped, still cloaked in shadows. She *knew* what Gil and Wev would want her to do.

She just did not know what *she* wanted to do.

Jeltor charged into battle at the head of the group, Shinigami and Barnabas flanking him and Gar running behind at the back of the diamond. Jeltor's suit had panels that could unfurl to make him a giant shield and the team had used this as best they could.

As soon as they started to get to the point where it would not matter any longer, Barnabas and Shinigami threw themselves as far to the sides as they could, vaulting from their cover into the fray before the robots could re-target.

Barnabas knew that whoever was using these warriors had not practiced. They had not gone through the admirals' training and passed it. They did not have what it took.

Unfortunately, they still had hundreds of robots at their disposal and thousands of bullets flying each minute, and they might win by sheer luck.

That royally pissed him off. He *hated* it when people won by luck instead of skill.

Gar had climbed onto Jeltor's back and now vaulted over the Jotun's head and deep into the ranks of the robots. He, like Shinigami and Barnabas, was determined to wreak as much havoc as he could, and he did it admirably.

Within the dense ranks, grenades were thrown, and the robots did not react quickly enough to quarantine them. Blasts rang out, Jean Dukes were fired, and there was the occasional yell of Barnabas or Gar catching a hit—bullet or mechanical fist.

They were better, Barnabas kept telling himself. He dispatched his enemies with brutal efficiency, always circling to the outside of an encounter so that only some of them had a clear shot at him. He kept taking them down, chipping away at their numbers, washing them away as water would wear away stone...

And yet, water was one of *his* problems. The level was still rising, and it was slowing him down. He struggled to move as quickly and predictably as he needed to. Currents made things even more tricky, and he could not easily tell where the walkways ended and the reservoirs began. More than once, he fell under the water and emerged cold, escaping a robot by luck alone.

Luck. A battle should never come down to luck.

They were still pressing forward, but the injuries were beginning to take their toll. Shinigami had been hit often enough that parts of her machinery were not working as well as they should. Both Gar and Barnabas, despite their healing, were in pain and cold. Jeltor's suit had taken damage far beyond where he should have bowed out of the battle.

"Who...the fuck...*are* you?" Barnabas yelled toward the back of the chamber.

"I am no one, *human*," the voice spat. "I am nameless to you. When I am gone, no one will think to look for me. No one will know what truth you were seeking. There never was another black ops team, was there? It was all a lie."

"It was your panic over it that proved it true," Barnabas called back. He barely missed stepping into a reservoir again and choked on a mouthful of water, swearing silently as he pried the sensor panel off a robot and ripped its gun arm off for good measure. "If they haven't come yet, they *will*."

"They won't," the voice snapped, "because they won't have a chance. It will all be over too quickly."

There. There it was, their entire plan. Barnabas didn't know the how of it, but now he knew their goal.

And he knew they thought they could achieve it.

"Your people will never stand for this!" he yelled back. "Never, do you hear me? You are the worst of them, and they will revolt against you and show every other species that they did not want this. They will defeat you from within."

"Oh, no, they won't." The voice was far, far too satisfied, and the water began to rise much faster. "And while I'd love you to see it, I think it's better if you don't live that long. It's been a good fight, human, but it's time—"

The voice cut off, and Barnabas, who'd been climbing on top of a robot to stay above the water level, noticed that the waters had stilled as well.

"Hello?"

He looked around. Jeltor had activated something that allowed his suit to float, and Gar and Shinigami had done the same thing Barnabas had.

And there, at the end of the room, perched on the shoulders of another biosuit, crouched the slim shape of the assassin. She nodded her cybernetic head in greeting.

"Hello again."

"Hello," Barnabas replied, surprised into politeness. "So who was that you just killed?"

"And why did you do it?" Shinigami added. "You waited quite a while to intervene. He's been distracted for quite some time."

The assassin laughed, an eerie sound. "Who it was doesn't particularly matter. As to why..." She paused as she stood. "It was what you said about the Jotuns rising and showing the universe that they weren't a part of this. You don't mean to destroy us when you learn the truth. I see that now."

She leaped—into the rafters.

"So I'll do you a favor," she called down, her voice echoing. The waters began to recede. "Look up the Infrastructure Revitalization Committee."

There was the sound of a door closing, and she was gone.

"That could be boring," Gar said, but the rest of the group was distracted by Barnabas' laughter.

"A committee," he said helplessly. "I always knew committees would destroy the world. Well, let's all go get patched up. We have some committee-hunting to do."

B arnabas took a restrained sip of juice and closed his eyes in pleasure. "Ah. Truly excellent."

"Most people would gulp it down," Gar told him.

"There is value in self-control," Barnabas replied gravely.

"Don't listen to him," Shinigami stated. "It's the stick up his ass talking."

"I do *not* know what that phrase means," Gar complained.

"You don't need to," Barnabas said wearily. "Suffice it to say she's insulting me."

"Teasing. I'm teasing. I do it with love." She looked at the food. "I wish I could eat this. You all seem to like it so much. Tabitha says these are some of the best sandwiches she's ever had. I've...cleaned up the sentiment somewhat."

"We'd guessed that." Barnabas smiled as he took another sip of juice. "So. It is time to decide our next move. Normally, I would wait until we had eaten, but we cannot afford to waste any time."

"I've asked Aebura and Kelnamon to look into any attacks on Ubuara or Brakalon colonies, and to report any other unexplained happenings," Tafa said. She had jumped into the role of chief researcher eagerly, networking with other biological organisms.

"That will make my predictions and assessments better," Shinigami agreed. Once Tafa had collected the research, Shinigami set to work crunching the numbers. Together, they made an incredible team, and what Shinigami could do with data, Tafa had a talent for "seeing" in another way—her artist's eye could sense a distortion in data, and once she pointed out what she saw, Shinigami was often able to make sense of it.

"As far as I can tell," Gar said, "there haven't been any attacks on Luvendi settlements, mainly because there *aren't* any Luvendi settlements. I think we'll have to look at it another way. I've put very vague calls out to the Luvendi I know to see if they knew anyone who dropped out of contact unexpectedly. The best way to get Luvendi would be to hire them into roles in a remote company and abduct them from there. The network on Luvendan itself is far too strong for people to vanish without a trace."

"Let Tafa and Shinigami know what you find," Barnabas said with a nod. "We'll have to see if we can find any Torcellans to work with."

"Try Gor'rathi," Shinigami suggested. "The Gerris Station administrator. He owes us some favors."

"In a manner of speaking," Barnabas murmured. "There were only problems on the station because of us."

"You're not enough of an opportunist," Shinigami told

him disgustedly. She shook her head. "Any word from Jeltor, by the way?"

"None yet." Barnabas fought a wave of worry. While Jeltor's family had remained at the safe house, Jeltor had gone back to Jotuna to begin spreading the word among the Naval captains. Whatever committee this was, they had to find out more about it.

Jeltor was filled with a renewed hope that there would be trustworthy members of the Senate, and Barnabas, despite his caution, was inclined to agree with him. Surely many senators had gotten into politics with an intent to do good work—and surely there were still some who had not been corrupted or jaded.

They just had to find them.

"We'll stay here until we get word," he decided. "There's no place safer for the *Shinigami*, and we can see our friends. I wish there was something to do, but there isn't until we know more."

"You could help Elisa," Shinigami suggested.

Barnabas looked at Carter's wife, who was making her way out of the kitchen with two trays of food. She looked a bit more tired than usual but was otherwise in very good spirits.

"Is there something she needs help with?"

Shinigami smiled, and Barnabas was reminded of how much those cybernetic eyes could see. "She's pregnant again," she said quietly.

"Why didn't you say so earlier?" Barnabas was up like a shot, taking one of the trays from Elisa while the rest of the table looked on in amusement.

"Good things happen here," Tafa said. She looked happy

and was almost in awe of this place. Tethra, on High Tortuga's smaller continent, was not a place of elegant buildings or big money, but it *was* a place where people greeted each other happily, and loving care showed in the construction of the buildings.

"It took a lot of work to make it this way," Gar told her. "A lot of courage." There was a lot of history in those words.

"Some of that courage was yours," Shinigami told him. "And we'll do the same with the Jotuns. I promise. No matter how dark it seems."

"And so," Grisor said, "while Biset's death was tragic, it has served as a valuable warning to us and has destroyed one of our most dangerous enemies. He bought us safety at the cost of his life so that the Jotuns might rise to lead all the species of the universe—as we were ordained to do!"

He shuddered and rippled with the force of his words, and the other committee members, each floating in the tank with him, bowed down before him respectfully.

Grisor, as he looked out at the assembled group, wondered if any of them truly believed the words he said. For certain, he had no grief over Biset's death. Biset had been a powerful committee member, ruthless and willing to do whatever was necessary to preserve the committee and advance its goals. He was the one who had suggested using Huword, and that had been an excellent suggestion, indeed.

But Grisor did not particularly care that Biset was dead.

It was one less potential loose end, one fewer person fighting for power when the committee's aims were finally reached. Biset would have ordered them all killed and taken over.

Grisor—who was planning to do the same, of course—was not sorry that Biset was gone.

But in every worthy enterprise, there was an element of danger. One must find allies, and allies could be dangerous, unreliable, and power-hungry. A good ally *was* all those things because worthwhile people always were.

When the rest of the committee rose to look at him, Grisor saw that they thought the same way. None of them cared about the rhetoric. Oh, they would pay lip-service to it. It would not do to have someone overhear the wrong speech. When the Jotun people heard what had happened, they would need to have a good, noble reason for supporting it.

If they did not? Well, they could be convinced. The experiments had shown that conclusively.

"Let us discuss progress," Grisor continued smoothly. "As you know, we have lost Huword. Therefore, we will need another source within the Navy. Fortunately, we have the means to turn any of them to our side now."

There was a flood of approval, chemicals rushing sweetly to him in the shared tank.

It had taken hundreds from each species to get to this point. Some species were still difficult to convince. The mind was a complex thing, after all, and not easily controlled. Each species had its own failings and weaknesses.

But the Jotuns they had figured out early on. Now the

committee had the strength to make any Jotun loyal to them.

And very, very soon they would have planets full of aliens, each turned not only into slaves but loyal slaves—and the Jotuns would rule this sector, unassailable.

"Who will we choose?" one of the committee members asked. "Which admiral is best placed to convince the others?"

"No," another argued, "we should choose the one we can get to most reliably."

"We will not choose from among the admirals," Grisor countered smoothly.

Everyone looked at him.

"When word gets out of Huword's dealings, there will be a crisis of faith. No one will be above suspicion."

They all waited.

"No one," Grisor continued, "except the one who exposed Huword and the Senate in the first place."

A few understood, but not all. He marked them; they were weak links.

He explained, "There is no other logical choice but Captain Jeltor. And luckily enough, he's on Jotuna right now."

FINIS

AUTHOR NOTES - NATALIE GREY
WRITTEN OCTOBER 9, 2018

Thank you for reading Justiciar! I can't wait to launch into this next part of Barnabas's story - what started as a murder investigation is part of something much, much bigger, and Barnabas and his crew are going to be tested in ways they've never imagined...!

I want to offer an extra-big thank you to the whole team this time, starting with Michael, who was vigilant and caught the first signs of burnout after a very productive spring and summer. He encouraged me to take the necessary time off, and Lynne, Steve, et al. really helped make it work. Thank you so much! Thanks also to Jeff for the lovely cover. I'm so glad we get to see Shinigami now!

I couldn't do this without the beta readers, both the first-round set (Sandy, Jim, and Sam) and the JIT group. Thanks for the typo and canon checks!

And thank you, as well, to B and L, who are a joy to me every day.

Sincerely,
Nat

Before I explain what is going on, let me say THANK YOU for not only reading this book, but these author notes, as well.

Today is Tuesday and I'm in Frankfurt Germany, attending the Frankfurt Book Fair – the largest in the world. I choose to come here as a company to understand what the bigger market looks like, to make relationships happen, and to see a few fans here in Germany.

We came in a day earlier this year (we arrived hours before the first meeting last year, a very poor operational choice for sure.)

Because of this better life choice, I actually got out of bed in time, and enjoyed the opening meeting.

Further, I got a chance to speak with a representative of a research company based out of the UK that is more connected with Trad (traditional) publishing than indie. I did this to see if we have options related to helping show the growth of markets with Indie Publishing numbers. Since they (trad pub) don't have any insight into our sales, and Amazon isn't about to supply them, they are doing some heavy scraping of the site via a 3rd party to understand the size of our genres.

While part of me is concerned that better insights bring additional competition, I realize that companies of their size and abilities could help grow the market bigger, so that we all benefit.

Because of this mornings meeting(s), I have NEW business ideas and hope to be here next year, writing another Author Note discussing something new that caused my little brain between my ears to quiver in anticipation.

Who knows? Perhaps I will be fortunate enough to break a whole new country open for Sci-Fi and Urban Fantasy.

I might get a t-shirt like the one that says 'I'm a big deal in <insert country.' ;-)

Hehe.

Below is a duplicate from another author note (TUMB 11) – HOWEVER – it is important for those who enjoy Fan Pricing.

Ad Aeternitatem,

Michael

--- FOR THOSE WHO HAVE NOT READ THIS IN BROWNSTONE #11 Or JUNTTO ---

LMBPN has set this BHAG (big hairy audacious goal) of releasing 400 titles next year. To make this happen, we had to get a cracking and bang a few brain cells together to figure out how to streamline our process.

Which, you know, was probably said last year, but I didn't FEEL like being responsible last year. As the owner of this company, I didn't want to be told when I had to have stories in. The whole concept made the obstinate part of my personality stand up and try to figure out who to flip off.

In the end, I had to give myself the finger.

Way to fuck yourself over, Michael.

Why? Because it's one thing to have two or three (at most) books coming out in a week. But, when we started doing full weeks of books (well, five days, not weekends) the challenges exposed themselves.

One of the issues is fan pricing. How do we continue the pricing, and reduce the effort because with 400 books, we have a LOT more to do and emails are a serious time and effort constraint, and we already sent too many.

FAN PRICING ON SATURDAY's

We are moving to releasing our books at $3.99 (a $1.00 less than regular price) during the week, then on Saturday's pricing all new releases (except box sets) at $0.99 for Saturday. On Sunday, they go up to regular price.

This way, you always know what day to look, and we are able to send 2 emails during the week focused on book releases. One on Sunday / Monday that announces what books are coming out (and when) for those who (for whatever reason) don't care and then again on Saturday with the books, and the links to the Amazon website (we don't always have this a week before.)

We are HOPING to have more content on the LMBPN

Publishing website about interesting stuff that might apply to you (including games, Anime, backstory on stories and authors etc.) When we get this running, we will release a special Wednesday email to highlight our blog posts.

Soon, I will be reducing my Author Notes in the back of collaboration books. There is no freaking way I can put out 500 word (or more) author notes in the back of 400 books. So, my plan is to do a Mad-Libs sort of feature where the core is consistent, and I can add in one or two unique items and see how that goes.

Making 2019 happen at 400 books is a mountain type goal for me. I suspect in 2020 we will reduce the number of books released, as we take what we learned in 2019 and cut the chaff.

However, for those that follow us, we appreciate your shouts of encouragement as we try to accomplish something (to my knowledge) NO Indie Publishing Company is doing.

Bring it on, 2019, bring it on!

Ad Aeternitatem,

Michael Anderle

BOOKS BY NATALIE GREY

Shadows of Magic

Bound Sorcery

Blood Sorcery

Bright Sorcery

Set in the Kurtherian Gambit Universe

Bellatrix

Challenges

Risk Be Damned

Damned to Hell

Vigilante

Sentinel

Warden

Paladin

Justiciar

Writing as Moira Katson

Shadowborn

Shadowforged

Shadow's End

Daughter of Ashes

Mahalia

CONNECT WITH THE AUTHORS

Natalie Grey Social

Email List

https://landing.mailerlite.com/webforms/landing/w0k9j4

Follow Natalie on Amazon

https://www.amazon.com/Natalie-Grey/e/B01MYG7K8P/

Facebook

https://www.facebook.com/Natalie-Grey-393234677682987/

Michael Anderle Social

Website:
http://kurtherianbooks.com/

Email List:
http://kurtherianbooks.com/email-list/

Facebook Here:
https://www.facebook.com/TheKurtherianGambitBooks/